YOU'RE IN THE WRONG PLACE

Made in Michigan Writers Series

GENERAL EDITORS

Michael Delp, Interlochen Center for the Arts
M. L. Liebler, Wayne State University

A complete listing of the books in this series can
be found online at wsupress.wayne.edu

YOU'RE IN THE WRONG PLACE

Stories by Joseph Harris

WAYNE STATE UNIVERSITY PRESS

DETROIT

ISBN 978-0-8143-4808-6 (paperback)
ISBN 978-0-8143-4809-3 (e-book)

Library of Congress Control Number: 2020938984

Publication of this book was made possible by a generous gift from The Meijer Foundation.

Wayne State University Press
Leonard N. Simons Building
4809 Woodward Avenue
Detroit, Michigan 48201-1309

Visit us online at wsupress.wayne.edu

CONTENTS

And of that second region will I sing,
in which the human spirit from sinful blot
is purged, and for ascent to Heaven prepares.

—Dante Alighieri, *Purgatorio*, Canto I, 4–6

Jack

Would You Rather

On my twenty-first birthday, Ken bought me a Jameson and told me to start putting hair on my chest, laughing through his smoker's cough about how his sons were too soft to work the punch, how his daughter could kick my ass. Ryan, that suave pretty boy who always fixed his hair in the greased window of his CNC machine, bought me a Stoli, told me to start watching my figure. Billy, eyes following his Keno numbers flashing across the TV behind the bar as carefully as they scanned the odds in the *Free Press* while he sat by his laser cutter, bought me a 7 and 7, told me to get lucky. Matt, all bullshit testosterone and bulging back muscles from five years at the shear, bought me a Slivovitz, slapped my shoulders, reminded me to go to Mass in the morning to thank God if I survived the night. Jim and Ben, whiskered veterans of the press room, bought me a Budweiser, told me to pace myself, muttered something about the separate trajectories of their namesake sons, and went home to their wives. Brad, the welding department's resident philosopher, bought me a Jägermeister, made me toast to Karl Marx. Dennis, Mike, Steve, and Harry, the rabble-rousing fucks that they were, so notorious for pranks they were banished to the four corners of the shop, bought Four Horsemen shots for all of us—Jack, Jim Beam, Johnnie Walker, and Jameson—and while I tried to keep them down, they told me that it was about time I got my tolerance up and started hitting the happy hours around Ferndale with them. And last but not least, Peter, my haggard comrade in deburring, hanging on longer than everyone, stalling for time, not wanting to go home to the wife he didn't love and the kid he didn't want, bought me a shot of Rémy Martin, told me to savor it, that it might be the last good drink I ever took.

Then, Jess's head on my shoulder, her hand on my leg. "Would you rather have a Pom Bomb or a Lemon Drop, Jack?" Her favorite shot or mine.

"I think I'd rather have a water." I felt clever, giddy, like I always did with her.

The bartender shouted something at Jess. She leaned in to whisper, "Would you rather have ice or no ice?"

I balanced awkwardly on my stool. Jess—and the room—spun around me. I brushed her dirty-blonde hair behind her ears, focused my eyes on hers.

"No ice." I kissed her on the forehead. "Let's go swimming."

"We have all weekend for that." She reached into the pocket of her jeans and flashed the keys to her aunt's cottage that she had gotten for my birthday weekend up north on Lake Huron.

We were all at Kady's Bar on Nine Mile, halfway between John R and Hilton Roads, where, girded against the blight of other shops, Dynamic Fabricating stood, lucky possessor of one of the last defense contracts in our inner-ring Detroit suburb of Ferndale, manufacturing all the parts of an armored personnel carrier for the wars six thousand miles away. My place of work, employer to two shifts' worth of shearing, deburring, pressing, welding, and machining sons of bitches—and all the sordid bastards drinking to my health.

"Happy birthday," Jess said, and we kissed among the crack of scarred pool balls and garbled baseball scores from the plasma TVs and a sloppy, off-key karaoke rendition of Bob Seger's "Feel Like a Number."

It is my favorite memory, and it haunts me now.

Jess let me sleep in, packed up the car without me, filled the tank, grabbed us coffees, jerky, and trail mix from the gas station, then chocolate and champagne from the convenience store across the street.

"How's the head feel?" she asked, pulling open the curtains.

"It hurts." I dragged the covers over my head.

Outside the open window of our bedroom, September bloomed ecstatic, exhaling summer's final breath over the roaring diesel engines on I-75. Inside, empty moving boxes and Jess's textbooks from her night classes at Wayne State covered the floor.

"Would you rather have aspirin or Advil?"

"Surprise me," I said.

Jess opened the drawer of the bedside table, sifting through paystubs for plastic bottles. "You get your check yesterday?"

"Shit . . . guess I was too eager to celebrate."

"We'll swing by the shop and the bank before hitting the freeway."

"What's your hurry, anyway?" I asked, tossing off the sheets, fingers circling Jess's spot.

She crossed her arms. "I thought you were hungover?"

I stood up, cupped the small of her back. "Thank you for last night."

"I was a good sport." She ran her hands through my hair, smoothing out drowsy clumps before we embraced.

Sex when you're in love is like talking without speaking—bodies and breathing synching before collapsing, drunk with bliss. It is more than intimacy, and when we caught our breaths that morning I think I realized, for the first time, how people could grind through routine, the utter mundanity of labor, to pay for a life with someone who is a reflection of their better self.

These were our early days together, where everything seemed to be a running conversation, when we were always in proximity, as fascinated by each other as the day we finally met.

Although we'd gone to high school together, I'd never talked to Jess—captain of the softball team with a 3.6 GPA and out of my league. Besides, I was sure I wouldn't find the words to articulate feelings I couldn't define. We actually "met" at Dynamic—she was filing contracts in the office, and I was starting off in deburring, grinding off the jagged edges of steel pieces cut from the laser and sheets of aluminum clipped from the punch. I'd waved at her without reciprocation during lunchtime, watching her leave for the Double EE Restaurant with the rest of the office as I waited for the food truck to pull into the parking lot so I could choke down a wet turkey sandwich.

I finally got a chance to talk to her at the Hazel Park Carnival the weekend before Memorial Day in Green Acres Park, a few blocks northeast of Dynamic. The whole shop went—an all-expenses paid reward for a month of sixty-hour weeks. We wound up next to each other at a water-gun game, trying to pop a balloon with a plastic Uzi.

"Good luck," she said as she eyed her target.

"I don't need it," I said, faking suave.

She cracked a smile and pushed my arm as the bell rang.

"No fair," I said. "I didn't see the rules."

She won, handily. The proprietor walked her over to the prizes: cheap, plush apex predators with toothy smiles.

"Would you rather have the crocodile or the jaguar?" he asked.

"That's an alligator," she said.

"How can you tell?" I asked.

"It's tiny." She examined her suitors. "Alligators are tiny crocs."

"I never knew that," I said.

"Someone didn't pay attention in biology." She tucked the alligator under her arm.

"How about a victory meal?" I asked.

"You don't want a rematch?"

"There's no shame in second place."

As we walked through the midway toward the food carts, sporadic fireworks shot from the bungalows around us, hissing and bursting in the thick spring air.

"Would you rather have an elephant ear or a corndog?" I asked.

"You're buying?"

I nodded, trying to hide my grin.

Over cotton candy and Icees, Jess said she'd always wanted to tease me about the indolent flop of my hair; that I should've built up the nerve and talked to her sooner. I told her what passed as my philosophy: that things work themselves out if you give them time and space. She told me about the night classes she'd finally saved up for, that her ambitions weren't constrained to carnival games—she wanted to be the first person from her family to graduate from college, then get a master's in counseling so she could teach the kids from our neighborhood that ringed Dynamic that they could do whatever they wanted as long as they worked for it. I told her I thought work was immaterial—something we had to do to pay for life outside of it—feeling the air vibrate between us. Then we waltzed from cart to cart, chewing caramel apples and kettle corn, trading horror stories about our exes, laughing until we snorted. We ate until our teeth throbbed from sugar, then tried to stump each other with classic rock questions as the flashing lights of the midway colored our faces: *Would you rather see the Who in '69 or the Stones in '72? Would you rather live in London in the '60s or New York in the '70s? Would you rather go to your place or mine?*

And as our days together became weeks, it became our motif—would you rather, choosing between trivialities that provided the opportunity for us to goad, to laugh, to fall in love. Friends at work told us to cool it, to be careful, but we couldn't. We were spending every day then every night together, so after my first raise, I got a low-interest loan and bought a two-bedroom shack three blocks from the shop, and Jess moved in.

Dynamic was quiet, which was eerie—I'd never been on the floor without a pair of green foam earplugs to soften the deafening thuds from the shear or the precision grinder's metallic cries. Jess and I walked through the chipped bay doors in the back toward the filing office in front that looked out across Nine Mile.

"I've never been in your office," I said. "I've never seen what you do during the day."

"You want a tour?" She opened the door of the office, turned on the lights. "This is where the magic happens."

It was a large, beige room roofed by fluorescent lights. Floor-to-ceiling filing cabinets, bulging with contracts, were separated by a few small, metal desks covered with pencil jars, rulers, and old desktop computers.

Jess walked me over to hers, picked up a contract, pantomimed turning on her monitor, before walking to a cabinet by the front windows, near the receptionist's desk, where my paycheck sat. "Just do that a hundred times a day," she said, putting my paycheck in her purse. "Come to think of it, I've never taken a tour of the shop floor." I took her hand and led her out of the office to the shear, a massive version of the scissors we used on construction paper for grade school art projects. "It starts here," I said, mimicking the motion of Matt's arms before launching into a history of the shop as told to me on the floor.

Dynamic didn't start in defense. Like all the other shops on the east side of Ferndale, Dynamic was founded after World War II and supplied auto parts for the Big Three auto companies. After the Japanese and Germans rebuilt their auto industries (*with our goddamn money*, my grandfather used to say) and started eating away at their market share, Dynamic adjusted and adjusted and adjusted again, eventually winding up in defense work, which they'd been doing for ten years by the time I joined.

From the shear, I walked Jess through the fabrication process: the punch, where Ken dissected aluminum sheets into rectangular pieces; the laser, Billy's job, which cut elaborate patterns out of steel; deburring, my department, where the excess metal of the resulting pieces was ground off with belt sanders and hand tools; the press room, where Jim and Ben inserted the smoothed pieces into massive calibrated presses and re-formed them; welding, where Brad, mask lowered, melted the folded pieces together in a haze of acrid smoke; and machining, where Ryan washed and drilled the welded product one last time before they were inspected, boxed, and shipped to be finished with a chemical treatment or a coat of paint.

When we reached the shear again, I handed Jess a fender from a half-full shipping box. She turned it over with her hands. "It's crazy to think we're made of the same stuff."

"What? Steel?"

"Well, carbon and iron make steel, right? They're both in us—a part of us."

I took the fender back from her and studied it, puzzled.

She grabbed it back, tossed it in the shipping box, and pulled me to the back door. "We'll discuss it in the car."

We took my check down Nine Mile and deposited it at the bank before Jess drove her rusty Grand Marquis up all four levels of the neighboring parking garage—the highest point in the city, where we went during that summer's rainbow sunsets: softened light trapped by the hazy dome of carbon that compressed it into outrageous hues of purple, orange. From our vantage point, those evenings and that morning, the neighborhood was a leafy, pungent grid of warehouses and industrial shops surrounded by two-bedroom bungalows and dotted with postage-stamp parks. The borders, roughly, were Hilton Road to the west, I-696 to the north, I-75 to the east, and Eight Mile to the south, bisected diagonally by the CN train yard and horizontally by Nine Mile. To the west, the rest of Ferndale: bungalows in the southwest, stately two-story brick colonials and knock-off Tudors sprinkled with bars and restaurants in the northwest along the Woodward Corridor. To the north: Pleasant Ridge, Royal Oak—the verdant Oakland County suburbs. To the east, Hazel Park and Macomb County—a network of fading blue-collar cities that emptied out into Lake St. Clair. And to the south, the sprawling enigma of Detroit that ended at the river and Windsor, Ontario.

Our eyes drifted, as they always did, toward Dynamic, sitting in the industrial artery that spread southeast from the intersection of Nine Mile and Hilton.

"Isn't it pretty?" I asked. "In its own way."

"More than Lake Huron?" Jess asked, pulling at the bottom of my shirt, urging me back to the car.

I-75 was empty when we left Oakland County, giving a salute to the giant portrait of Christ on the side of the Dixie Baptist Church in Clarkston.

"Which apostle would you rather follow?" I asked from the passenger seat. "Peter or Paul?"

"I don't get to pick James?" Jess asked.

"Those aren't the rules." I rolled down my window, felt the pulses of country air cool my forehead.

"Paul," Jess said.

"Says the Catholic." Treeless fields flew by us, the tall grasses waving in the breeze. "He's more interesting, don't you think? He used to hunt down Christ's followers."

"Peter was a fisherman, a man of the people. He had a more glorious death. Founded the universal church."

"Maybe we should analyze them as historical figures?" she asked. "I should do that for my theology class."

I turned and reached into the back seat, looking for a candy bar but finding only Jess's weathered philosophy textbook. I picked it up and fanned the pages, stopping at a dog-eared page.

"What's materialism?" I asked.

"You want to move on from the saints already?"

"*Physical matter is the only fundamental reality* . . . the fuck's that mean?"

"We covered it in class last week. It's a philosophical concept that says that all that ever has and will exist, including our own bodies and everything we think and perceive, is the result of the interaction of matter." She rolled her window down, let the wind push her fingers back. "It's kind of what I was talking about earlier, at the shop."

"Well . . . so what? What's the purpose of studying it?"

"If it's true, then religion can't exist, because if matter is all everything is composed of, then there's no mystery in the world. There can't be anything spiritual, so God can't exist. Or an afterlife."

I shook my head. "That's bleak."

"It is." She took a sip of coffee. "But it's probably true."

I stared at our reflections in the rearview mirror: shaggy hair we cut ourselves to save money for furniture and cheap sunglasses from a gas station in Trenton, bought after a day of thrifting for appliances Downriver.

I held her hand. "That's a good one, actually."

"What is?"

"Would you rather believe something you know isn't true but helps you get through day-to-day life or believe something you know to be true but makes you feel like shit?"

"Fuck," she said. "That *is* a good one."

The cottage was clean save a few trash bags filled with empty beer cans sitting in the screened-in porch. I dragged them to the garage while Jess unpacked, flipping through our itinerary and laying out sunscreen and beach towels. After putting the champagne and chocolate in the fridge, I looked out the kitchen's solitary window at the gravel road winding through the pine trees that opened up on the hard, blue canvas of Lake Huron. We grabbed two beers from the fridge, jumped back in the car, and drove to East Tawas for a late lunch. We rolled down the windows and drove eighty up US-23 yelling every chorus from Neil Young's *Everybody Knows This Is Nowhere*, which blared distorted from the tape deck. We locked eyes as we traded verses, turned away when the choruses returned to scream them out our respective windows that pummeled us with drafts heavy with the musk of newly fallen leaves. And it hit me, then and for the first time, how good this all felt after months and months of work.

I didn't know what I wanted after I graduated from high school. I just knew what I didn't: a windowless cubicle in some airless suburban office park, wearing a tie every day; I didn't want to go to college either, paying money I didn't have to sit through crowded lectures about things I'd never care about. My high school counselors told me a bachelor's degree was the new diploma—that if I ever wanted a real job in the economy that was coming, I had to suck it up and get one. At the insistence of my parents, I took some classes at Oakland Community College, clearing out prereqs until I got my associate's degree while doing roofing part-time with my dad until his jobs started drying up (*Shouldn't be this slow during spring*, I remember him saying) and I became unnecessary. After a summer on the couch, my dad called around and landed me an interview at Dynamic. Jess handled my paperwork.

Dynamic was hard—both on Jess and on me. Five thirty in the morning until four in the afternoon, with a half day every other Saturday. The work could get monotonous—Jess's endless trips from her desk to the filing cabinets matching the same balletic motion of my hands turning a jagged piece of metal around a belt sander—but if you had half a mind, you could zone out for the hours between breakfast, lunch, and close. When I started, I tried to conjure some ambition for myself or run through the forward lines of the Red Wings' Stanley Cup teams from the late '90s. When Jess and I started dating, I just thought about her. In October, it would be my one-year anniversary there, and I'd be moved (or so I was promised) out of deburring and into the press room. That meant another raise, which meant that, after a few months of cooking dinner and staying in on Friday nights, I could buy a ring.

In the car, Jess grabbed my hand as the dueling guitars of "Down by the River" poured out of the open windows. I pulled her hand to my mouth, kissed her ring finger.

Jess slowed the car to a crawl, and we slid into East Tawas, the afternoon light turning the windows of the Newman Street storefronts into mirrors. We parked and admired the essentials of a northern Michigan downtown: the chocolatier, the second-run movie theater, the used bookstore with its display of beach reads. Jess took my hand and we walked to Barnacle Bill's, her favorite restaurant. We put our feet on the brass rails and eased into the torn leather seats at the bar and ordered the endless fried smelt, chasing them down with pitcher after pitcher of cold, cheap beer. We traded gossip from the office and the floor, who was pissed at who and for what reason, made off-color jokes about the fielding and pitching abilities of the company softball team (*We would've won more if they let me pitch every game*, Jess said). We ate and drank and talked and laughed until the Tigers game started on the TV behind the bar.

"Fuck," said Jess, "we've been here for three hours?"

"Time flies," I said, reaching for the check.

Jess snatched it from my hands. "You can get dessert."

We stumbled into the twilight, walked to the ice cream parlor by the beach, and bought waffle cones filled with cherry chocolate chip ice cream and rainbow sprinkles. We took off our shoes and walked down the pier licking our sticky hands and nudging each other into the paths of noisy seagulls.

When we reached the lighthouse, we put our feet through the railing and bit off the soggy edges of our cones as the sunset splashed shades of orange on the lake.

"Remember our conversation on the drive here?" Jess asked.

"Maybe," I said, putting my arm around her shoulders.

"About believing something you know isn't true?"

"Oh yeah. That."

"You answer first."

I finished my cone, brushed caked sand from my feet. "I don't know if it matters."

"Of course it does," she said. "It shapes everything you want."

"Elaborate."

"Most of my family doesn't think this life is the *real* life, you know? They think it's a trial, a test to get into the real life when they die."

"I never thought of it that way." That was true—I was happy listening to the serrated harmonies of crickets and train whistles on the back porch while Jess filled the margins of her textbooks with notes.

"But I've never believed that," she said. "I think this is it."

"What's wrong with that?"

"I dunno . . . if you have the materials to create your own meaning in the absence of God, you're free. But if you don't, you have to work to acquire them, like we have to, and if you can't work . . ."

She looked away, faced the vacant beach.

"I don't know if you remember, but the night we met, you said that, at some point, everything comes down to making money. I guess I'm worried about how I'm going to pay for it all—pay for the life I want."

I reached for her hand. "How *we're* gonna pay for it all."

When the sun dipped below the horizon, we stood up and walked back to the car.

When we parked backed at the cottage, Jess bolted from the passenger seat and ran toward the lake. I stopped in the house and grabbed the bottle of Cook's before following her, the gravel from the road denting my soles. When I reached the lake, Jess had waded in up to her knees, the moonlight turning her hair a silken gray. I walked out to meet her.

"Where's your suit?" she asked. The water was still warm.

"Where's yours?"

We took off our clothes, rolled them into soggy balls, and tossed them on the shore. We slipped beneath the surface, and I uncorked the champagne and we passed it back and forth in the shallows.

"You know what the guys told me to sing at Kady's last night?" I asked as constellations blanketed the darkening sky.

"How would I know?"

"'Beast of Burden.'"

"Oh my God," she said. "I love that song."

She backstroked out toward the slivered moon, singing the first verse between submersions.

I sat on the rocks in the shallows, shouting back the chorus.

When we finished the song, she floated back to me. "Last question for the day."

I swam to meet her. We put our hands on each other's bare legs for balance, feeling the goose bumps bubble to the surface. "Better make it a good one," I said.

"OK . . . everything I've been talking about today . . ." She took a pull from the bottle, looked at the stars. "Would you rather . . . no, *do* you believe it, or not?"

I pulled her close, resting my chin on her shoulder. "Believe what?" I stared out across the water, drank in the moonlight as it spilled unevenly across the gentle tides made by our bodies.

She turned her head until our eyes met. "Look up at the stars."

I did, then looked back into her eyes.

"You think we're made of them?"

"And nothing else?"

"And nothing else."

"Let's not think about it." We kissed, tasting the accumulation of the day on each other's tongues. "Not tonight."

"OK." She ran her hands through my hair, smoothing out the knots. "Not tonight."

We kissed again before going under, together.

That's the last memory I want to have of her—of us . . . of myself. I've done my best to forget, but here's what I remember: when I checked my voicemail as we drove south of Flint on I-75 Sunday night, sunburned after a long day at the beach, I heard the floor manager telling me to sleep in and come in at nine the next morning.

When I did, the CNC machines were turned off, the air hoses silent. They had the folding chairs and coffee out like they usually did for safety videos, but they'd wheeled the TV into the office.

The boss came down from upstairs, hands in his pockets. Some investment bank in New York, he said, wasn't bailed out by the government, by me or Jess, Ken or Ryan, Billy or Matt, or Brad or Dennis. We sat stone-faced in a semicircle as he said something about mortgage securities, the credit markets tightening, that our last contract hadn't been renewed, that there was enough work left for two months, maybe three. This wasn't just affecting us—he said he'd talked to his auto industry friends, who told him they were almost out of cash.

"If any of you are religious," he said before letting us go for the day, "now would be the time to pray."

Over the next year, everything in the neighborhood seemed to follow Dynamic out of business. Every day I drove résumés to the handful of shops still open all over the east side: to Hazel Park, Warren, Roseville, Fraser. When that didn't work, I spent every morning in the queue at the temp agency before they waved us away. Jess floated us on her student loans, using them to pay for groceries, gas, the mortgage, but after a year she dropped out and took up waitressing until the local Coney Islands and sports bars closed, too.

After cancelling our internet, we spent our mornings at the library perusing Craigslist for gigs, only finding day-long landscaping jobs for twenty dollars that were filled by nine in the morning, and our nights at the kitchen table sorting through past-due notices.

Our friends from high school whose parents bought them a way out came back from the coasts for Thanksgiving, telling us about college life, internships—how exciting it was to live in vibrant places, the possibilities they held. We went home and heated canned food and pulled further apart, away from each other, into ourselves.

After a while, we were fighting every day, taking our frustrations out on each other, the would-you-rathers mutating into did-you-remembers, have-you-checked, where-have-you-beens. It would have been easier if we had some distance to ease the pressure, but there was nowhere else to go.

We tried watching love-conquers-all movies, couples fighting against the odds in dire straits: *Breakfast at Tiffany's*, *The Gift of the Magi*, *Brassed Off*. While watching *It's a Wonderful Life* on Christmas, sitting on opposite ends of the carpeted space that once held our couch, I began to realize that love has a price, or it exacts one, and that love needs materials to sustain itself. Just as we wanted to work, but couldn't, we were willing something we both wanted but couldn't save. I began to think that if you didn't work—or couldn't—then you didn't need to exist.

On Memorial Day, two years after our first date, I gathered all the beer cans festering in the basement and fed them through the recycling machine at the liquor store. I ironed my blue Dynamic work shirt and shaved off my beard. When Jess came home that night, I pulled the $10 bill from my front pocket and asked if she wanted to go to the carnival. She sat down on the floor, pulled her hair behind her ears, shook her head.

She didn't have to say anything—we were too exhausted to fight each other. I watched her pack her bags—the same ones she once stuffed with quilted blankets and Coppertone and cheap champagne. As she slept in our bed for one last time, I leaned against the walls of our empty living room, trying to think of one last thing to say, one last thing to remind her of what we had. I tried to stay awake until morning, but when the slant of the afternoon sun roused me the next day, I opened the blinds and her car was gone.

When the interest rates on my mortgage kicked in that fall, I lost the house, too, and moved back in with my parents.

I never called the guys from Dynamic—none of us tried to stay in touch. Every time we saw each other at the Kroger or the liquor store or wandering the parks aimlessly in the middle of our empty days, we were bereaved again, kept distant by the collective silence of our own inadequacy.

Besides, after a while I didn't drink to celebrate anymore. I drank to hide. I fucked near-strangers on Friday nights just to escape, for a few minutes, the gnawing banality of my life. I missed Jess, but what I missed more was not feeling claustrophobic—like I couldn't get out. Like I was trapped.

I did see her again, on my twenty-fourth birthday. I didn't want to be alone, so I walked down Nine Mile to Kady's Bar, sat on a stool, looked for familiar faces, sipped some cat-piss beer. It was the first time I'd been there since we split up because Kady's was Jess's place, and because we didn't have physical assets, I thought I'd cede it to her.

I was making small talk with the bartender when she walked in with someone else. I waited for my gut to sink, and when it didn't, I longed to feel something other than indifference. As I watched them pick out a table and stare blankly at each other, I thought about our car ride to Lake Huron, about Jess explaining materialism, and I thought I could see my life never moving from my barstool, just fading into nothing.

We made eye contact and I lifted my glass. She excused herself from her table and walked over, eyes on the sticky floor. We made small talk, Jess looking just below my eye line, as if she were staring into the guilty stubble of my cheeks, and I kept thinking: This is it now? After we've laughed and wept and screamed . . . after we've consumed each other?

"You look good." Jess, lying, always trying to cheer me up.

The bartender came over to take our order.

"You have any specials?" I asked.

Jess put her hand through my hair, smoothed the greasy knots.

"Would you rather have a shot or beer?" he asked us.

"So," I said to Jess, "what'll it be?"

KATE

Don't Let Them Win

My brother Pat called me and said we had to drive to Ann Arbor and get our other brother, Kenny. I told Pat I wasn't interested. Ever since Kenny's girlfriend left him for that Econ professor in January, Kenny had turned strange, dissolving, for the first time in his life, into booze. I said that I had repeatedly called and tried to get him to visit me in Chicago, that I would pay his train fare, but he'd drunkenly call me a sellout, bougie, fake—throw the whole hipster vernacular at me. I told Pat that I had driven to Ann Arbor to visit Kenny around Valentine's Day, but all he did was sit in his room, drinking Popov and watching YouTube videos of giant centipedes eating tarantulas, and say things like, "Crunchy, right?" We left his room once to go to a show his noise band was playing at the Blind Pig. Halfway through their first song, he threw up all over his bass guitar and passed out on stage. I heard some girls next to me say, "Oh my God, how hot is he?" and all at once became conscious of the wasted time in life that you never get back. After I had carried him back to his bed, laid him on his side, and brought him a glass of water and a trash can, Kenny looked me in the eye and said, "Don't fucking judge me, Kate. You have no idea what this feels like." Then he passed out.

"He cleans himself up, and I'll be the first one there," I said.

"That's why we need to go," Pat said. I could hear the pulse of his bleeding heart though the receiver. "He needs help."

"So it's intervention time?" I asked, not disguising my fatigue. Kenny had become Pat's latest passion project. When Pat's girlfriend left him the previous year for some "New Detroit" venture capitalist, he moved to Corktown and got involved in "community-oriented urban revitalization," as he called it. When he came to Chicago for St. Patrick's Day, he drank club soda with lime and talked my head off about rezoning and blight restoration as I took shots of Jameson with my friends from work and narrowed my view on the single guys draped in green beads swaying back and forth around the bar. He told me the next morning over breakfast that he didn't mean to come off as judgmental, but that since I'd moved to Chicago, my lifestyle had become increasingly selfish, my worldview more cynical. I told him I wasn't going to apologize for being the only one out of the three of us to choose the path of pragmatism before the recession, and that middle-class kids bringing a new kind of colonialism to Detroit was just as selfish as working in commodities—more so, I said, because at least I was being transparent about it.

We hadn't talked since then.

But after five more minutes of Pat's nudging, I told him, "Fine, I'll fly in tomorrow. But you better have those *we're here to help you, not judge you* statements written for the both of us." As I hung up the phone and gazed across the Chicago skyline, I realized that I had planned to come home to see our dad anyway—the fabricating shop where he'd worked his whole life had closed three years ago, and he was still struggling with the transition to forced retirement. We'd have a chance to reconnect and shake our collective heads at the two other fools who completed our family.

On the plane back to Detroit, I flew over the rusting plants of Gary, which always made me think of home, of my dad underneath his yellow '73 Dodge Dart on Sunday afternoons with his ashtray and beer can on the ground within reach, Mick Taylor's guitar solos from *Sticky Fingers* leaking through the speakers of his cassette radio. He would call me in to help him change the oil or rotate the tires and use the time to give me advice on the romantic world I would someday enter.

"Don't let 'em see you cry. Don't let them see they can hurt you. If you do that, then they've won, which is all they want in the end. Trust me."

After mom left us, he kept a routine, working the early shift at Dynamic Fabricating Monday through Saturday, showering and cooking dinner for us, retiring to the garage to smoke his L&Ms and drink his beers, flipping through the used boat classifieds for an upgrade to the Chris-Craft Cyclone we had at our place on Harsens Island. On Saturday night he would walk down to the bar and bring back a tired-looking blonde divorcée, and I'd try to sleep through the squeaking mattress coils coming from his room. Sunday morning he'd cook breakfast for me and Pat and Kenny and the woman. Then he'd walk her out to her car, kiss her on the cheek and say, "Till next time," but it was never the same one twice. Then we'd walk down Woodward to St. James's for Mass, and after we walked back, he would throw on a dirty striped shirt and slide under the Dart.

After mom left, every week was like that, a routine so religiously followed I forgot what our lives were like before it. My dad never talked about it—there were no pictures of her on the kitchen table or hanging on the walls of his work area in the garage. Sundays were our day together, the coach and future player going over the potential pitfalls of being left behind by someone you trust. I listened as I watched Pat and Kenny play street hockey or freeze tag through the garage's solitary window, laughing and running as their sweat mixed with the carbon fumes from the few shops still open in the industrial corridor off Hilton Road.

"Romantic love's a pain in the ass," my dad would say. "It tilts your head away from the only thing and person you should care about." I just nodded and looked down the driveway toward the street, biding my time.

"How's business?" my dad asked from behind the wheel of the Dart.

"It's business, Dad. Same shit, different day. You know how it is."

"Knew." He lifted his mesh fishing hat, ran a veiny hand through his gray hair. "Not sure how to fill the days now, Katie." He knocked his other fist on the dashboard. "Can only work on this piece of junk so much."

"Go shoot pool at Kady's." I looked over at him, smiled. "You're retired now."

"Don't remind me." We wove through the twisting airport roads that spit us out onto I-94 East. "You have lunch plans? Thought we could hit Loui's for a pizza."

"I wish. Pat and I are going to get Kenny."

"Is he still bitching about that girl?"

A teenage boy in a car to the right leered at me. I rolled my eyes. "Seems that way."

"Sometimes I think I should have spent more time with those two. Kenny especially. They're both soft. I trusted you to toughen them up, you know? To watch out for other people, what they want . . . what they're willing to take."

"Or leave."

He looked over and smiled, wrapped a calloused hand around my shoulder. "I'm glad you got out of here, Katie. But I miss you."

When we reached the curb in front of our house, he tossed me the keys. "Get that brother of yours home. He's too young to be so upset about something like this."

I parked out in front of Pat's apartment building on Michigan Avenue and waited for him to come down. I took in the ruins of Michigan Central Station and watched people play catch in the vacant weeds of the demolished Tiger Stadium. Hipsters shuffled between bars and coffee shops. They all looked like Pat, who, a few minutes later, came down holding a manila folder filled with loose-leaf paper, and I could tell from a distance he had written them on a typewriter.

"What happened to your computer?"

"Wasteful and unnecessary," he said as he tossed the folder through the window into the back seat. "I try not to indulge in the excesses of American capitalism."

I was glad I was wearing my sunglasses so he couldn't see my eyes roll.

"You wrote my 'statement,' I hope," I said as I started the car.

"Yes. Ours are distinctly different in tone, though. I felt a good cop, bad cop approach would be the most effective—you know, the most convincing."

"Who's playing who?" I asked, smiling. Pat just sighed and handed me scribbled directions to Kenny's.

I picked up I-94 West, and we rode under the overpasses and out of Detroit, passing miles and miles of small post-war bungalows, the wet autumn grasses rising through the blight.

"Can I ask you a question, Pat?"

"Of course," he answered with trademark earnestness.

"Don't you ever get tired of living somewhere so ugly?"

"I think it's quite beautiful in its own way," he said, defiantly. "Before our grandparents took the coward's way out after the Uprising in '67, it was the most beautiful industrial city in America." He rolled down his window and let the quick bursts of freeway air style his mane, shaggy for the first time. "You might appreciate that if you hadn't moved to a center of predatory finance."

I wanted to tell my brother what his ex-girlfriend thought about all of this, having left him for someone who perfectly resembled it. I bit my tongue instead.

"It's cold for October," I said.

"I don't mind," he said.

"I dunno, Pat." I listened absently to some prematurely drunk caller on sports talk radio. "Chicago winters are so miserable that I don't mind warm falls, Indian summers."

"Well, it was warmer this fall," Pat said, a smile making its way across his lips. He told me about his involvement in the Occupy movement, about camping out in Campus Martius in downtown Detroit for two weeks, how everyone had helped each other expecting nothing in return, the late-night rallies, the clinics set up for first aid, for the sick. He went on about how different it was, unlike anything he had seen growing up with me and Kenny in Ferndale, the Saturday house parties in East Lansing, how the thought of redefining the concept of capital and being involved in direct democracy had altered the way he looked at the world.

"Didn't the bums steal all your iPhones?" I asked.

He shook his head and looked out the window.

We slid through the empty freeway, taking in the sparseness of Wayne County, the fading blue-collar ideal of Allen Park, Taylor, the places my dad told me to get away from during the Sundays under the car I now drove through to bring his baby back home.

When we were young, Pat used to ask me if I missed our mom, and I said, "Sure," but in truth I couldn't remember her. I remembered the day she left only because of how quiet it was after, having gotten used to the screams seeping under closed doors. We were all born within a year of each other—a production line of Catholic mistakes. I was four when it happened, and I think my dad confided in me not so much for being the oldest, but for being the final link—visually, intellectually—between my mother and him. No matter what I told Pat or Kenny—about being independent and pragmatic and cautious in their trust—they rejected it: Pat with his bleeding heart, Kenny with his technical virtuosity, his dexterity over a strung fret. And so were set the pairings: my dad and I, Pat and Kenny. I tried again and again to explain to them the intricacies and difficulties of the matters of the heart as taught to me by our father, but their dismissiveness was their way of rebelling.

I made friends from the neighborhood and our public schools, some of whom also came from single-parent houses, and, being from one myself, they were easy to spot. They kept me at a distance, unwilling to confide in me and exhibiting visible anxiety when it came time to part ways on our respective streets and say goodbye.

By the time we got to high school, boys became the obsession—who was dating whom, who was cheating with whom, who was heartbroken and who had done the breaking. My friends were vocal about their exploits, chiding me when I didn't discuss my own experiences and experiments. I told them it was none of their business, conducting my affairs with stealth—answering folded loose-leaf notes with winks and subtle tilts of my head—and consummating them quick and hot in back seats and bathroom stalls. Unlike my dad, I sometimes had the same one twice if he was skilled enough or discreet enough or as frustrated with his situation as I was. I remember one of them lingering in the passenger seat of my car, hands behind his head, smiling. He told me how "different" I was, how "cool" it was to be with someone who dated "like a guy."

"What's that supposed to mean?" I asked.

"You know—guys are supposed to pursue girls, take them out, buy them stuff, convince them they're not scumbags."

"And then what?"

Nervous, he changed the subject, going on about how I had a kind of viciousness that felt emasculating, like the bad girls on TV shows. I told him TV wasn't real, at least not its idealized notions of wanton chivalry masquerading as some antidote to sexism.

That's when I knew what I wanted to do: make enough money so that I could decide the rules of romantic engagement for myself, and I knew that I could never do that in Detroit.

My brothers could not have been more different. Whereas I had played sports, Pat started fundraisers, and Kenny got into music, starting his own three-piece band. Whereas I had cherry-picked lovers I could easily dismiss, Pat gravitated to the girls from broken homes who always looked tired and wore hand-me-downs from their older siblings while Kenny seduced the foreign exchange students and shy girls with variations of "Wild Horses" on his acoustic guitar. Apart from our hair and our eyes, it would have been difficult to ascertain that we were related at all.

"Turn here, onto 23," Pat said. I blinked and refocused on the road.

I let out an audible sigh as we parked in front of Kenny's house on Catherine Street, a block east of Community High. I lived in a dump during my junior and senior years at Kalamazoo College, but Kenny's place was worse. The grass was shin-high, the rotting steps bordered by untrimmed bushes. The door swung half-open behind a creaking, useless screen stuffed with cigarette butts and joint ends. When we got out of the car, I looked east down Catherine Street at the students coming and going to and from class. I walked up creaking, nearly breaking steps to the porch, which was lined with empty plastic handles of Ten High.

"How romantic," I said.

"Just stop." Pat shook his head and turned the doorknob.

I made my way up the stairs as I had done a few months before, bracing myself for a familiar sight. Pat followed close behind.

Kenny's room was empty. I waded through empty beer cans and consignment store shirts soaked in vomit to the window, which I opened to lessen the wretched stink. Pat sat on Kenny's bed, then stood back up. He rubbed the back of his pants and brought his fingers to his nose.

"Urine." He shook his head.

I made myself a clean spot and sat down on the floor. "Just like when he was little."

"What?"

"After he was potty-trained. When he still wet the bed. Dad tried everything."

"He was too impatient."

"Dad or Kenny?"

"Very funny." He stretched out his arm and waved the fingers of his hand. I looked around at Kenny's boozy squalor, and when I looked back, Pat was wiping tears from the corners of his eyes.

"What's the matter?" I asked.

"I just feel so bad for him. He . . . he really cared about that girl, you know? He was nothing but good to her, and . . . and . . ."

I stood up and brushed away flies swarming around a moldy sandwich.

"It's just a girl, Pat, for the love of God. Nobody is dead. He's got his youth and his health and is good at something creatively." I picked up the sandwich. "There is no reason for *this*. So *stop* it. Everything is going to be fine."

"It's hard for him to see that now. Maybe if you'd been hurt before . . ."

"Maybe there's a reason I haven't."

I heard him mutter something under his breath when the door swung open and Kenny stumbled into the room. Pat jumped up and caught him before he hit his head on the bedside table. He reeked.

I stripped off his bed sheets and laid some dry clothes in their place. Pat eased him down.

"Well, look who's here," Kenny said, smile creeping across his lips. When they opened, I saw that his teeth were stained with nicotine.

"How are you, bud?" Pat asked. "Thought we'd bring you back for the weekend, you know? We could catch up, just like old times."

"Patrick," Kenny said. "Paaaat-rick . . ."

I shook my head. "Kenny, goddamn it, it's three o'clock."

"Yeah, but it's five o'clock somewhere." He curled up into a ball, his face pale and gaunt. He reached behind his pillow and produced a forty-ounce bottle of malt liquor. Pat wrestled it from his shaking hands.

"Let's eat something first, OK?" Pat asked.

I couldn't believe these were my brothers, had no idea how they had been reduced to this. Everything I had listed off to Pat, all the reasons in the world to open Kenny's eyes, were totally useless—as useless as Pat's motherly soothing.

"You don't have to do this to yourself, Ken," I finally said.

"Who asked for you to be here, anyway?" Kenny asked, staring at me with red eyes.

"Pat here thinks we need to save you."

Kenny laughed. "That's a good one. You guys don't need to save me. I just need a drink."

"You need to stop acting like a child," I said.

"You're a child." Kenny laughed.

I shook my head. "What a waste of time."

"Wow. Look at the big shot. Mrs. Big City Big Shot with all the money is just so much better than her stupid little brothers—"

"Enough," I said.

"—her stupid little brothers who would just *embarrass* her in front of her big-shot friends—"

"No wonder that girl left you! Dad was right about you, Kenny—you're too soft for anyone to care about." It cut through the room, leaving a piercing silence. I could hear birds singing outside the window.

Pat opened his manila folder and gave me a piece of paper.

"Oh boy," Kenny said, drunkenly unfazed. "A story."

"Kenny," Pat cleared his voice, "we're here because we love you, and we're worried about you."

Pat nodded in my direction. I looked down at my pages.

"Your behavior over the past ten months has been," I tried to keep myself from exploding again, "*concerning* for both of us. You're coming home with us, right now."

Pat nodded his head and smiled at me, then started reading again.

"We'll all be home for the weekend together, on Breckenridge. We could cruise Woodward in the Dart, maybe take a trip . . ."

Kenny sat upright and exhaled, his face suddenly ashen.

"You guys care that much about me?"

We nodded.

Kenny stretched out fully on the bed and hung his arms and legs from the sides.

"Then carry me home. Carry me, servants." *This* was Kenny, my baby brother.

We carried Kenny down the stairs, his limbs comically limp. I sat him upright in the back seat as Pat settled in next to him.

"Just get some air," Pat said, rolling down the Dart's manual windows. "Some fresh air will feel great." We rode down Main Street to the freeway, watching the undergrads carry hampers full of dirty clothes to the laundromat. It hadn't been that long ago for me, those college years in Kalamazoo: I had taped breakup letters on dorm room windows, laughed at dinner invitations, seen those hollowed looks boys get when they're rejected by someone they don't just want to fuck.

The first time I met Pat's ex-girlfriend was during my first year in Chicago, when I drove to East Lansing for the Michigan–Michigan State football game. When Pat introduced us, he smiled broadly and held her by the small of her back. I never understood why she was the one he wanted to settle down for—she was pretty, ambitious, dressed well, nice to him, but nothing special. During the tailgate, I told him I guessed that that was what happened when you decided you were tired of being alone.

"It's not like that, Kate . . . you don't really *choose* them," he told me, watching her play horseshoes with her friends. I wanted to debate him, tell him everything our father should have, but Kenny arrived with a guitar player from Michigan's Residential College. She had a nose piercing and dyed-pink hair, and he spent the rest of the day playfully teasing her. Kenny told me that night, coming out of a bedroom shirtless, that the only way to know someone, *really* know someone, is right after you make love.

"Haven't you ever felt that way?" he asked me around a bonfire later.

"I've never wanted to."

Kenny sighed and stared into the fire. "Do you want to meet her?"

"Meet who?"

"The girl I brought with me. She's tough—I think you'd like her." He smiled. "I know I do."

Looking in the rearview mirror, I remembered I hadn't met her that night or known if she was the one who had broken his heart. I had never even asked. I tried to locate my shame before I realized I hadn't felt it in years.

"I know how it feels, Ken. I know how it feels." Pat was holding Kenny by the shoulders. "You let them inside you so much that they become you, that the two of you exist as one person. And when that stops, arbitrarily, cruelly, there's that gnawing hole . . . I'm still trying to fill it." He dried his eyes on his shirtsleeve. "Was it the same for you?" When Pat looked down, he saw Kenny passed out, drool running from the side of his mouth.

For some reason, I became furious. "For Christ's sake, Pat, enough."

"Enough of what?"

"You two are so stupid, you know that? And not just Kenny. You say you're being progressive about your breakup, but I think you're full of shit. If you said anything to me about rebuilding that corrupt rancid shithole of a city before nine months ago, I would have remembered it. And even *if* you are somehow convincing yourself that what you're doing down there is good or in some way has value, you're doing it for yourself and no one else. You're doing it to get over that girl or to make her jealous."

"What would *you* like me to do?" Pat's voice was lower, distant.

I knew I had an answer, something that would help him, help Kenny— it burned a hole in my memory, and I leaned forward when I finally remembered.

Don't let them win.

"That's what Dad used to say: 'Don't let them win.' Don't let the people you love hurt you. That's what you're both doing. You're letting them win. They left you guys because they wanted something more than what they thought you could give them, and now your pain's all over the place."

"Sure worked for Dad."

"What was that?"

"You want to say Dad never changed after Mom left? That he never hurt?"

"He didn't." Deep down I knew that wasn't true. A bubble of anger grew in my chest.

"Who do you think he bought this car for?"

Then there was a *pop*, and the Dart shrugged to the right with a flat.

Pontiac Trail was empty as we waited for AAA.

Pat leaned on the hood, staring at the neon lights of a distant gas station. "We should call Dad."

"When the tow truck shows up. No use in wasting his time." As the minutes rolled by, I thought about this family, *my* family, my two pathetic brothers with no ambitions but to stay home and fall in love. And they wondered why they got hurt, as if everyone just wants that, a life in a post-industrial dump where all you have is love—all you have is your family. And these two here, one drooling, one crying, looking to *me* as if I have all the answers, as if I'm their mother . . .

"If you had only looked out for yourselves . . ."

"What was that?" Pat asked.

I said it again. "If you just looked out for yourself . . ."

And I thought about who had said that to herself twenty-three years
ago.

Forget my dad, she was saying it to me. She was saying, without
speaking, that she did not love me enough to try to make it work.
That although I loved her and needed her, the feeling was not mutual, and so
everything ended and there was nothing I could do about it.

And my dad, putting on that face every morning and every night, my
dad, going through the motions in the wake of his abandonment, every
day having to see me, who must look like her, have her eyes, the living
embodiment of their stagnant love. My dad, telling me to be tough and
look out for myself so I didn't wind up like him. Like I was always so
much *better*.

And here I was, all those years later, thinking the same thing about
my brothers.

"I'm sorry," I said. An image of my mother rose before my mind's eye,
and I needed her again . . .

And then I blinked and it was gone, my mind trained, as I had so
rigorously trained it, back to judgment and scorn. Hate was my vaccine.
It always had been.

"Sorry for what?" Pat asked, eyes on the road.

"About . . . about your work. It must be hard . . . shouldering something like that, trying to help people who got left behind. You'll do just
fine."

That was true. Pat would make it, wincing, taking his life farther from
mine.

"What are we going to do about Kenny?" he asked. Kenny's head
shifted from left to right in the back seat, lost in a dreamless sleep.

"He'll be all right."

And I hoped so. I hoped he wouldn't keep drinking, hoped he wouldn't
get some easy girl and use her as a vessel for his sorrow, hoped that when
she left him he wouldn't move from drink to drink and place to place in
that rotting state, losing his ability to do something beautiful, hoped he
wouldn't wind up back on our street drying out with our dad, even though
he did do all of those things. Maybe when he reads this he'll understand

that I understand and that I'm sorry, that beyond anything else it is the essence of primal betrayal that lingers and never really goes away.

And I thought of our dad, back in the garage doing another repair job on the car he bought all those years ago for the woman who abandoned us: how he and I had let her win.

RYAN

Exit, Stage Left

My Uncle Mark was the black sheep on my mom's side. He moved to Windsor during Vietnam, saying, "Good luck with that bullshit war—I wanna live." When he got back, he hustled the pool sharks at some eastside Ferndale bar and made so much money that he bought a double-wide on Harsens Island, two hours north of Detroit, and never came back. My dad and I would go up there for a week every summer and Uncle Mark would drink too much Canadian Club and smoke too many cigarettes while watching reruns of *Snagglepuss*—an obscure *Yogi Bear Show* segment about the misadventures of an ebullient pink mountain lion—and telling everybody what was wrong with them.

He pissed off everybody; that's what he was good at. I always found it funny. I mean, the only reason he did it was to get a rise out of people, and you'd have thought they'd catch on after a while and just roll with it. I always belly laughed, and I'd like to think he appreciated that, like some washed-up comedian homing in on the one son of a bitch in the stupid, bloated crowd who appreciates his act.

So, it didn't necessarily floor me when he dropped dead at fifty-eight from a heart attack after all the whiskey and Marlboro smoke, but it did surprise me when he left a cryptic note in his will for me.

"Let me read it again," my mom said after the funeral. "*For Ryan, I leave you the relic behind the holy water in my cathedral.*" She shook her head. "He's pulling your leg. Isn't this just like him."

The rest of the family said they didn't really care that Uncle Mark was gone because they didn't care for him, and that at least the holidays would be peaceful from now on. Christmas was a week away, and they chatted excitedly about the absence of tension, rudeness, and condescension from the Advent season.

After changing out of my funeral suit in my shabby apartment, I examined myself in my bathroom mirror, noting the curve of my shaved jawline, the definition of my abs, the bright blue of my eyes. *Time to make rent, you handsome devil*, I thought as I grabbed my car keys.

I wove down Nine Mile in the snow drifts, eyes following the lazy tango of the windshield wipers as I drove to meet my two o'clock appointment.

Holy water in his cathedral, I thought to myself after a tumble at the Red Roof Inn off the I-75 service drive. *The hell could that mean?*

"Maybe it's a metaphor," said the divorcée next to me, fingers in my hair.

"I don't think my uncle was that clever."

"Well, what was his God? Where did he worship?"

That's when I remembered the name of that bar where he'd hustled his slice of the American dream—Kady's Bar, by my old shop. I'd been there, years ago, for some coworker's birthday party. "It's probably there. Worth checking out, at least."

She pulled a twenty out of her purse. "Got time for a quickie?"

No Save-A-Lot groceries for me this week, Uncle Mark, I thought to myself as I went down on her. I could almost taste those Kroger rotisserie chickens.

See, after my fabricating shop closed, my plan was to get some headshots and move to New York to do some modeling. I hitched out there with some kids I knew from high school—a shoegaze ukulele band with dreams of a write-up in *Pitchfork*—and wound up walking around Manhattan for two weeks, no bites on the line. "Great body," I was told, "but your face is too kind—you look like you're listening to someone's problems. I need someone who looks like they're going to jack my car" (I took it as a Detroit jab, let it slide). I didn't want to go home right away, not ready for the *told-you-so* looks at the unemployment office, so I started hanging around the bars in Williamsburg, Greenpoint, watching lonely Rust Belt ex-pats drink Canadian Club and kicking off an unexpected bed-hopping tour of Brooklyn (a rent-saving tip Uncle Mark bequeathed to me on those Harsens Island summer nights when my dad was out of earshot). In bed, the women told me that all the guys in Brooklyn were selfish assholes who never really enjoyed sex or knew how to please anything other than their own egos—that they never listened or even pretended to care that the person whose intimate company they just enjoyed might have an interior life. I told them it was different in Detroit because we couldn't afford to be mean, and they said, "Oh, God, Detroit, I'm so sorry," like it was a fucking leper colony. That's what I remember about those salad days in Brooklyn: the dirtiness, the bourgeois pity, how all the guys *were* pricks (although I guess rudeness is a turn-on in bohemia; toothless cruelty must be sexy in a contemporary *Dangerous Liaisons* kind of way). I remember how nice it was to really get to know someone after the anticipation of orgasm, how I should've charged for sex.

And when I got off the Greyhound back in Detroit, that's exactly what I did. It wasn't hard to find clients—all the wives of pink-slipped factory workers in the bars and parks and grocery stores around town were awfully horny—famished, *even*, as Snagglepuss would say. My boyish, nice-guy looks worked well in contrast with their gruff, angry spouses. I had a face they could confide in. One of them told me after a romp around her trailer in Warren that it was good thing I was young because marriage was really just a financial and hereditary agreement between two people who expect to keep making money, and that it was amazing how fast "love" dried up when bankruptcy was breathing down your neck.

So, I discovered there was a hole in the market I could expertly fill, and the fake allure of an eccentric gentlemen I gleaned from watching hours and hours of *Snagglepuss* with Uncle Mark went down terribly well—fabulous, *even*. I never got to tell Uncle Mark about my post-industrial enterprise, but I'm sure he would have loved another punk kid from his mutt bloodline making a dishonest living. I dreamed of making enough money to buy a house outright, maybe a cottage up north where I could grow my own food, be self-sufficient, live without money. Maybe I could shoehorn one of my tricks into coming with me, if we wanted the same thing.

• • •

"Club soda with lime," I said to the bartender, noticing the freshly buffed shuffleboard table, the yellowed photo of Tiger Stadium signed by the '84 World Series team. The place was empty.

"You in the program?" she asked, reaching for the soda gun.

"Nah. Just think it's boring." I didn't drink because it killed Uncle Mark, whom she didn't know.

"You think being drunk is boring?" She set the drink in front of me.

"I mean, it feels the same every time, doesn't it? I don't see the point in doing something over and over when you know the result's gonna be the same. Especially with those hangovers."

"So overindulgence isn't your bag?"

"I wouldn't say that, necessarily. I see everybody—especially since that mortgage thing stole everybody's equity, I still can't believe we didn't riot—spending all night drinking and then holding their heads and bellies all day until they can start drinking again. Living in a finite world and all, seems a waste of time."

"Well, what else is there to do around here now?"

"I'm partial to a romantic entanglement here and there." I picked out the lime wedge, sucked out the juice.

"Then why are you sitting in an empty bar at three in the afternoon?"

"So many questions." I winked—a good trick I learned from Uncle Mark when he was winding someone up on the Island, seeing if they would take the bait.

"Honey, you're the only one here. Gotta keep myself entertained." I thought her use of that endearment odd, since she looked to be my age. When she brushed her hair behind her ear and ducked into the light, I noticed the absence of lines around her mouth, of bags under her eyes.

"Do you happen to have Cartoon Network?"

"Wouldn't you rather regale me with tawdry stories?"

"Sorry. I don't kiss and tell."

"What a scam. Can you elaborate, at least? On your romantic philosophy?"

"Honestly, it's probably the only thing I'd do for money, though I reckon the ensuing loss of intimacy would . . . complicate my arousal. Problem is, ladies aren't too keen on fellas with no cash."

"Every girl? Is that so?"

"Is there anything I can do to make the questions stop?"

She leaned forward and met my eyes. "I know your con, boy. I've seen you around."

"I feel aghast—insulted, *even*."

"I knew it! The *Snagglepuss* bit, too."

"I don't think I've ever met a fellow *Snagglepuss* enthusiast."

She put one hand on her hip, gesticulated flamboyantly with the other. "For*sake*, and for*sook*. Heavens to *Bet*sy!"

I lowered my head to hide my laughter. "Where have you seen me? I haven't been here in years."

"A few times—the produce section of the Kroger on John R, chatting up a young mother of three as she pushed a baby carriage . . . in Green Acres Park, helping a housewife walk a fucking shih tzu . . . oh, Luxury Lanes on Nine Mile, giving a form demonstration to . . ."

"OK, OK . . . the cat's out of the bag."

"Not a bad hustle, I have to say."

"Enough about me. What do you do, miss. . . ."

"The fuck's it look like?"

"Sorry—I mean *did*. Before things went belly-up. I used to work at Dynamic Fabricating, that's why I'm curious."

She poured herself a shot. "I was a grad student in English at Wayne State. I was writing a thesis on economics and religion in the works of Steinbeck."

"I'm intrigued—fascinated, *even*."

"You can drop the *Snagglepuss* bit. Though I did find it charming when I first heard it."

"You did, huh?"

"Now it's you with the questions." She took the shot, traced the bar with her index finger. "Anyway, you'd be surprised how much 'God' and 'Christ' are evoked by a frustrated George as he juggles Lennie with the cold realities of private land ownership and slave wages in *Of Mice and Men*." She reached into the register and pulled out a fifty.

"What's that for?"

"I'm off from three to five." She winked.

"You have the wrong idea. I'm not some . . ."

"Oh, yes you are. Textual analysis teaches you to spot the intentions of the author."

"You don't seem like the type who needs to pay."

"It's been quite a dry spell. When my college fund dried up, I had to take this job and move in with my dad and brother. They're not big on . . . overnight guests."

I walked into the bathroom to take some "vitamins," making sure my performance wouldn't lag because I was still thinking about the funeral, about that line in Uncle Mark's will. I closed my eyes and tried to recall the last conversation I had with him on the Island, seeing if it could spit out a clue:

"On the Island there's this retired UAW guy who loves Bruce Springsteen, blares it from his pontoon whenever he's had too much beer. You know, all these songs about how great it was being young, all those broken dreams, winding up at the mill or foundry your dad always tried to steer you away from. Sentimental nonsense from some wistful drunk—makes me sick.

"And Ryan, all I can think is, *Fuck that guy*. Not just my neighbor, but Bruce Springsteen, too. If he could have seen what happened when those 'demeaning,' 'repetitive' jobs moved away, he would've written about something else. Like that work is so humiliating. Fuck's wrong with doing something eight hours a day? Especially when you're young. It's not like you're gonna do shit anyways. Only thing you *can* do is get enough money to do what you want till you die. Why do you think I love *Snagglepuss* so much? No other piece of American art has so perfectly defined the futility of the rat race, social climbing, bourgeois propriety.

"But *you* sure as fuck don't have to get that money slaving behind some belt grinder or drill press, son. That's for dumbasses like your aunts and uncles—like my neighbor with his fucking Springsteen. Use that brain of yours. And have faith in something—a tonic, something that gives you some clarity. Don't waste time on the misery. Growing up where you did, you see decay every day—you're surrounded by it. Life's a lot shorter than you think."

I cupped the pills and stepped into the stall. Carved over the toilet was Snagglepuss's famous departure: *"Exit . . . Stage Left,"* undoubtedly a memento left by Uncle Mark years and years ago. I reached out and touched it, moved my fingers through the jagged grooves.

When I walked out of the bathroom the lights were out. Near the back door I heard pulls on a cigarette, the jangle of car keys. *Tonic*, I thought. *Clarity . . . holy water.* I walked around the bar to the dusty liter of Canadian Club, pulled it out, and saw an envelope shoved into a gap in the cheap wood siding.

When I woke up, the sheets were warm. She smoked by the motel room window, eyes on the American flag flapping in the wind outside. "Looks nice against the winter sky, doesn't it?"

"Nice to see one out," I said. "A lot of them have been put away in the neighborhood."

"People are too cynical. Things don't go their way and it's *fuck this, fuck that*." She stubbed out her cigarette and reached into her purse. "What do you think about it here?"

This was the part that *I* would pay for: the pillow talk after you both release your tension and can nakedly be yourselves, at last. "It's not so bad. Would be nice to be able make some more scratch."

"No kidding." She walked to the bathroom mirror. "What else, though? What's keeping you here? I ask myself that every day."

"I guess I love the sensuousness of this place. I love the way it looks—the bungalows, the factories—I love the way it smells, with all the diesel fumes, the way it tastes . . . every time the seasons change you can taste the hidden flavors of Detroit. I love the sounds of semis on the freeway at night. Helps me sleep."

"How does it feel?" She smiled at me through the mirror.

I stretched out on the cheap bed. "I love this place the way I love sex, love intimacy, with all of the imperfections, the secrets . . . the history. But

I know it's not good for me because there's no way I can make enough money."

"That's the whole point of this country," she said, reapplying her makeup. "To acquire some capital. Once you do that, you can just own. You don't have to work."

"I think it's deeper than that," I said, admiring her figure in the mirror.

"If you don't believe that you're an idiot." She smacked her lips, evened out her lipstick. "Or a hippie. Or you're just rich. I get a lot of those kids in the bar, now. Grandparents got themselves some capital in the boom after the war. Then their parents went all hippie and liberal and now the grandkids are nihilists." She noticed me watching and moved back to the bed. "Horrible tippers."

"What about a cottage on some land up north—Lake Huron side, the budget side. Room for a garden, a few chickens. How much capital would I need for that?"

She laughed and kissed me on the forehead. "*Oh boy oh boy, George.* That won't run you much. Good luck getting a girl up there with you, though."

"I don't recall inviting you."

We wrestled, gently. She worked her way out of her clothes. "Wouldn't go anyway."

"And why's that?" I worked out of mine.

"You still believe in God?"

"Maybe."

"I don't. And if this is all there is, I want to be rich."

"You better get back to work, then."

"I'm not done yet."

We changed positions. I stroked her naked back. "For someone who doesn't believe in God you sure do take His name in vain a lot during sex."

"What are we gonna replace our orgasms with now?" She smiled at her cleverness. "Our *Oh Gods*, our *Jesus Christs*?"

"Maybe some Greek and Roman deities? *Oh Zeus! Mars! Athena!*"

"*Heavens to Murgatroid!*" She fell into me, laughing. "Religion is for the capital accumulation period, anyway—when you're sacrificing your existence so your children can piss the profits away. Once you have enough money, you can just stop believing."

She sounded just like Uncle Mark during Christmas Eve Mass. I kissed her neck.

"How do you want to die?" she asked.

"Does it matter?" I kissed her collarbone, the space between her breasts.

"To me, yeah."

"Just to drop, I guess. Fade away into nothing."

She pulled me inside of her. "*Exit, stage left* . . ."

When I woke up again she was gone. On the bedside table lay a few loose bills and some numbers scribbled on the motel notepad. I stretched out, walked to the bathroom, looked at my naked body in the mirror. Too skinny. Maybe I should charge more so I could eat more protein, I thought. I walked back to my jeans and pulled out Uncle Mark's $2,000 bar tab I found behind his holy water, setting it on the bed this pretty stranger and I had just shared our lonely moment on, Christmas lights from outside dancing on our stains.

I thought about the moment of *my* creation; how I understood people's sadness at Christmastime because of the love that lingers when the fleshy beacon is gone, when all that's physically left is some money or some debt, in one form or another. And maybe that *is* love, really—the ability of the dearly departed to give their still-living next of kin comfort, let them live in a way they couldn't or wouldn't. And maybe, just maybe, all those years down the line there'll be equilibrium, and everyone can forget about money and just get back to love.

But it was still early—enough time to make another hundred bucks, maybe two. I showered, put my clothes back on, and drove off into the night.

RICHARD

You're in the Wrong Place

When Glen didn't show up for work, we assumed he was out all night again, that he'd meet up after breakfast wearing his wraparound sunglasses, reeking of Skin Bracer to hide the smell. I'd thought about heading over to his house to rouse him, but I hadn't been there in years, and besides, I could barely see through *my* hangover. So Billy, Ray, and I poured Kessler into our coffee and toasted, "To Glen—fuck 'em."

Before this landscaping season, we'd been short on work since Dynamic Fabricating went under and took most of our clients with it—former Dynamic employees all.

Then in March, the bank that owned the property called. Wanted us to "maintain the grounds" of Dynamic until they could find a buyer. The first day on the job, Glen motioned me over to the front door with a languid swing of his arm. Someone had spray-painted: **IF YOU'RE LOOKING FOR WORK, YOU'RE IN THE WRONG PLACE.**

We thought that was funny as hell. Particularly the correct punctuation—probably some smartass who dropped out of college to get a paycheck, someone who thought all that "opportunity" talk about acquiring a humanities degree in a post-industrial economy was bullshit . . . someone like me, I guess, even though I would never have had the balls to tag the façade of some rotting factory.

In May, the bank called again: another contract to maintain the lawns of the foreclosed houses in the neighborhood—the houses of all our former clients. Standard cut, edging, weeding if there were gardens.

After downing the coffee, we stopped at a gas station to fill up the equipment and grab a few snacks. It took half the time without Glen harassing the attendant with his fucking lottery numbers. Billy walked out with a scratch-off, asked me to do the honors with his lucky nickel. I rubbed off the film and gasped.

"No way!" Ray said, chewing on an apple in his sun-faded U of M English T-shirt.

"How much, Dick?" asked Billy, lifting his dirty Tigers hat and running his hands through his greasy hair.

"Billy," I smiled and tossed him the loser, "if you're looking for winners, you're in the wrong place."

The first group of homes we hit was behind Dynamic and the train tracks that emptied out into the sprawling CN train yard. These were the rentals and starter homes, 500–700 square feet, two-bedroom bungalows with no garages. Even without Glen, we could do a whole place—front, back, edging—in under five minutes. We zigzagged through the neighborhood from north to south, stopping to sip coffee and eat Swiss Rolls behind the shuttered warehouses that faced Eight Mile.

"You worried about Glen?" Billy asked me, stirring in a ripped packet of Splenda.

"Can't tell if he's been hitting it more than usual," I said, though with Glen (and me, and Billy, I guess), it was always hard to tell. Landscaping attracts a certain kind of temperament. High turnover, mostly drifters with substance abuse problems (like Glen), or college kids working summers to save up for tuition hikes (like Ray), or burned out retail workers who couldn't stand another holiday season stocking perfume or selling vacuums making half of what they did at Dynamic (like Billy). After Easter you worked until the first post-Thanksgiving freeze, then started back up when the last March thaw turned everything to mud.

I loved the life—loved watching the seasons change, loved the camaraderie, loved that I could drink and gamble every day and no one said shit. That's why I dropped out of college—I couldn't stand the smugness, the elitism. I didn't want a fucking "life of the mind"—I wanted to work outside. Glen was my dad's drinking buddy, said he'd give me a shot in his operation. I took it, and for three years we fell into the rhythm: up at six, breaks at nine, noon, and three, punching out at six and staying at the bar till the Tigers game was over or Glen blew the last of the day's earnings on Jameson shots and side bets on pool games.

"That's just who he is," I said to Billy, who drained his coffee in one fluid gulp. "He's never been a morning person."

The clock hit nine, and the night shift at the only open warehouse walked out into the murky sunshine. Billy recognized one of them. "Johnny Boy!"

Johnny Boy shielded his eyes and walked over to us, his filthy sweatshirt billowing from the gusts of passing semis.

"This motherfucker used to work at Dynamic with me," Billy said, chewing the filter of a Pall Mall. Ray, as usual, buried his head in a yellowed paperback copy of *Capital*.

"So, how's this gig?" I asked.

"They got us on twelve-hour days, man. Fuckin' eight bucks an hour. Thirty minutes for lunch. It's borderline criminal, I'm telling you."

Billy swallowed a laugh. "Johnny, if you're looking for sympathy . . ."

I didn't know the prick, so I passed on the punch line, but Ray, ever eager to earn his working-class bonafides, chimed in, right on cue: "You're in the wrong place!"

We raced up Wanda to Nine Mile, then took a left toward Campbell Heights. The neighborhood was filled with overgrown gardens, grown mostly by Dynamic retirees who had seen their pensions sucked up when the owners filed for bankruptcy protection. We pulled out the pruners and the mulch and got our hands dirty.

We were clearing a shade garden when Ray noticed a bald man in a black smock walking an old lady up her front porch across the street.

"Hey, it's a fucking priest," Billy said.

Indeed it was. Ray wiped sod from his eyes. "Which one is he again? Father . . ."

"Fuck if I know," Billy said. "I stopped going after I got confirmed. That purgatory bullshit really rubbed me the wrong way. What a bunch of fucking nonsense. Besides, there's no way I'm nursing my hangover during Mass, you know what I mean?"

Ray called out to him. "Hey, Father!"

He turned to us. "Good morning, boys." He blessed us.

"Be nice, Billy," I said.

The priest adjusted his glasses, looked at me. "Richard? Richard Piscek?"

"That's right. How are you, Father?"

"I haven't seen you since your confirmation."

Billy laughed. "I bet this guy fuckin' baptized you, too," he whispered to me.

"He did," I said.

"Well, we'd love to see you at Mass again. People really need it since that factory closed."

"I'll go with you," Ray said, full of that Protestant fascination with my lapsed Roman faith. It pissed me right off, almost as much as having to take Glen to see his bookie on football Sundays if he was too drunk to drive. And where was he, anyway?

"All are welcome in the house of God," the priest said.

Billy couldn't help himself. "Hey, Father!"

"Yes, son?"

"If you're looking for converts, you're in the wrong place."

East of the factory were the bigger houses with bigger lawns—additions tucked into the front of the lots all the way up the sidewalk, fire pits surrounded by rusted folding chairs growing moss in the back. Edging out front took some time—so did pruning the fucking fire pits, throwing the rotten wood through our mobile chipper. I kept having to remove jams from Ray throwing them in too quickly and found dozens of scratch-offs. Probably Glen's or Billy's—that's the first thing they did with their paychecks every Friday.

When we reached the corner of Paxton and Cambourne, we saw three young guys dressed in black and red: a fat one with a snare drum, a lanky one with a sign, and a balding one with a loudspeaker. They were down from Ann Arbor on assignment from one of their Marxist professors, extra credit or some bullshit like that. Friends of Ray's apparently—they shook hands.

"We're protesting the unlawful seizure of this property and others like it," said the one with the sign.

"You don't say." Billy grinned, lit a cigarette.

"The capitalist superstructure is collapsing," said the one with the loudspeaker, "and with your help, we can usher in a better world for the working man." The one with the drum executed a low rattle of support.

I appreciated the sentiment, but I didn't need some smarmy U of M dickhead to tell me how fucked I was. These kids had never "worked" in the proletarian sense, and they'd never have to. It reminded me of myself a few years ago: a kid with a college savings account paid for by some grandparent's factory work—the opportunity to join the New Economy I threw away.

"Hey, kid," said Billy. "If you're looking for solidarity . . ."

I finished that one off; there's nothing I hate more than bourgeois offspring pretending to be Walter Reuther. "You're in the wrong place."

In the truck between houses, Ray went on and on about this event he was organizing for the fall semester back in Ann Arbor: some kind of town hall about the loss of faith and work in post-industrial society, how we lived in an indifferent universe, and how it all presented some kind of philosophical problem.

"So, let me get this straight," Billy said, draining a Gatorade. "You're saying that we gave up God when we got money, and that now that we don't got no money, we can't go back to believing because . . . why, again?"

Ray sat up, finished his last stick of jerky. Across the street, we made out a cadre of young DUIs riding their childhood bikes to the liquor store, still wearing their blue Dynamic work shirts. "Well, we've disproved the existence of another world, haven't we? But we can't disprove the existence of capital—it touches every single aspect of our lives, not just in terms of the financial but familial, even sexual. In unionized industrial societies, we could manufacture meaning through labor, creating wealth and purchasing the physical and emotional materials to build meaning without religion—a better life. But now, with religion gone and labor gone, what's left?"

When Dynamic went under, Glen and I were out at the bar after he'd lost $500 in a poker game to some local scumbag—Jerry was his name, I think—and Glen was telling me the difference between wants and needs. "Everyone who worked at that place, all they had was wants," he said, "all they had were dreams of what to do with that money. And now it's all fucking gone—now it's all gonna be needs from here on out." And as Ray went on about all his theoretical bullshit, I wondered if any of it would help Glen—help Billy, help me.

Billy didn't even wait till he was finished. "Ray, my man, if you're looking for transcendence . . ."

I decided to chime in again. The whiskey was wearing off, and I remembered how stupid I thought Ray was, slumming it up with us during his break from school, even though his family was poorer than mine. My dad never had to work at Dynamic—his did. "You're in the wrong place."

We went to the bar for lunch, chased our cheeseburgers with beer, and took a shot for Glen. On the TV some star-crossed lovers my age—arrogant young doctors or lawyers or something ridiculous like that—pleaded with one another that they needed time to sort things out; to figure out who they *really were.*

"Easy on the lotto tickets," I called to Billy. "Clogged the fucking chipper."

"The fuck are you talking about? I keep all mine. Sooner or later you find your pattern."

"That wasn't you?"

"Dick, my friend, if you're looking for advice . . ."

"Can we drop it for lunch, fellas?" Ray was sorting his money—his girlfriend was driving over from Grand Rapids, and they were heading across the river to Windsor for the night to go drinking and gambling, just like I did when I was nineteen. "It's kinda getting on my nerves."

"What would you know about nerves, college boy?" I sneered. The rich young lovers talked about their plethora of coastal opportunities, gesticulating theatrically that they *didn't want to live with regrets.*

"Must be nice," mumbled some bearded drunk next to me.

"Fuckin' right," I said.

"Can you imagine if someone started talking like that around here?"

I drained my beer. "If you're looking for self-actualization . . ."

"You heard the kid." Billy laughed from the Keno machine.

I tapped the drunk on the shoulder to buy him a shot, then caught a look at his face.

"Bobby? Bobby Kowolski?"

"In the fucking flesh." He put his head back down and snored. The bartender poured us shots and motioned with his head to a sign that said "The one and only rule: no sleeping at the bar."

"How the fuck are you?" I hadn't seen him since we graduated high school—must have been five, six years.

"I'm still here."

I put the shot in front of him. "Cheers, you son of a bitch."

He took the shot and perked up.

"I thought you were at Western?" Bobby had been the star point guard on our basketball team, got a full ride to college.

He pulled up his dirty sweatpants and showed me the map of scars on his knee. "Not anymore. Kept tearing cartilage. Flunked out after the injuries and got a job at Dynamic. Now I'm here."

The characters on the TV started crying. Billy walked over and put a hand on my shoulder. "So this is what Ray has to look forward to, huh?"

"Fuck Ray," I said, as Ray walked out.

Billy laughed. "Well, if you're looking for love . . ."

So it was just Billy and I hitting the afternoon houses to the south of Dynamic—the desperate ones, rotted and overgrown; the ones that were about to be condemned by the city.

The first one—added by the bank that very day—was really something: grass rising past my thighs, ivy crawling over the smudged windows, dandelions and clovers poking through the walkway gaps. It looked familiar, maybe one I cut a few years ago, but with my buzz on I couldn't remember.

I yanked the cord of my Weedwacker, and someone burst through the front door with an aluminum baseball bat.

It was Glen—sweat-stained shirt untucked, popped buttons exposing his distended stomach.

"Get *outta* here, you motherfuckers!" He went after the power mower first, Billy splitting as soon as Glen charged. He dented the hood then lifted the gas tank, smashed the engine. I dropped my Weedwacker and pleaded with him.

"Glen! Glen! It's fucking us, man! It's me!"

"You think you can just take my fucking property! Fuck you! I'll fucking wreck it all before you take it!" I tried to catch his eyes, but they were bloodshot without his glasses.

As he smashed the mower to pieces, I looked inside the house and saw hundreds of empty beer cans, some stuffed with scratch-offs, some with slips from the Hazel Park racetrack, some with parking tickets from the casinos downtown: Greektown, MotorCity, MGM. "Why didn't you tell me? I could have . . ."

"Could have done what?" He leered at me, cheeks slick with tears. "You ever have a fucking problem, kid? A *real* fucking problem?"

"Glen, put the bat down . . ."

"And how do you know my name? Who sent you here? You with Jerry? The credit card company? The fucking bank? Get the fuck off my property!"

"Glen, it's not yours anymore." I heard sirens down the street. Someone with a decent mortgage must have called the police.

"The fuck it isn't!" Then the cops pulled up behind him, wrestled him to the ground, cuffed him. The whole time he kept screaming, "You don't need it, you bastard, you son of a bitch, you don't need it!" and I could have sworn he was staring right at me.

With our stuff smashed up we went back to the bar. None of it was insured, so I thought I'd get drunk and not think about what we were gonna tell Ray tomorrow or how I was gonna pay *my* mortgage. On the TV, the Tigers were warming up for a West Coast day game. I felt around for the sweaty ball of money in my jeans and thought about needs. Bobby was still glued to his barstool, trying to stay awake. Billy tried to cajole me into a dart game, but I waved him off. I was too bothered by that thing with Glen to aim right.

I ordered another shot. Billy yelled something from the jukebox, but I couldn't hear.

I mean, where the fuck did Glen get off? Calling me spoiled. Sure, maybe I was, but not now—not thanks to him. Some cheerful Motown song drained out through the jukebox speakers, and Billy yelled, "Hey, Dick! You deaf? I said, 'If you're looking for work . . .'"

JUNE

Acolytes

Our father had been gone almost a year when my brothers started coming home drunk wearing identical coarse scarves wrapped around their heads like balaclavas. I made instant coffee, clipped aspirin coupons. I gathered the scarves from the floor and washed them in the cold cycle at the laundromat. When they started coming home drunk, bleeding, and bruised, when I was washing cuts with the last pulls of Murphy Oil Soap, I thought, well, they're really up to something.

They told me about a semi-pro soccer team of neighborhood kids, too dumb for the Division 1 colleges or too slow for Major League Soccer, who played their home games at the Hazel Park High School football field, part of a new state-wide league of teams from Rust Belt cities like ours. My brothers had joined the rabble of out-of-work boys cheering them on, hurling abuse at the visiting fans brave enough to make the trip before ambushing them in the parking lot afterward, fists curled tight around rolls of quarters.

I'll admit it: at first, it was great having them out of the house—summers in southeast Michigan you sweat through everything you own, the humidity like bathing in a sauna, and four boys in 700 square feet reek.

But the novelty wore off after a home game on Memorial Day. I watched them lift Salvation Army T-shirts to their bloody noses in our cramped living room whispering about how they'd been done by some kids from Port Huron and that they needed to expand their membership.

"Have you picked out a color for your costumes?" I asked Matt, Mark, Luke, Johnny—each one an imperfect reflection of our dead father.

"Green," they said in unison—the color of their team: Ferndale United FC.

Just like Ordinary Time, I thought as I looked at the bleeding Christ on the living room crucifix. "Don't the cops have an eye out for you now?" I asked.

"Relax, June," Matt said, his thick hands working his prominent nose back in place.

Mark wiggled a loose tooth in his nicotine-stained mouth. "There's no cops on the beat at night anymore—no money for it."

"Besides, we went to high school with all of them," Luke said. His receding hairline was flecked with blood.

Johnny, his pretty face purple with bruises, walked over and put a reassuring hand on my knee. "One of them even joined in last night."

"You acolytes have a name yet?" I asked.

They looked at each other, eyes alight. The name stuck.

Matt, the oldest, told me how incredible it was after an away game in Lansing as I dressed his wounds and spooned him Old Crow because his jaw was swollen shut. Not the violence, necessarily, but the thrill of its potential. When we were babies, Matt always told me that he loved my name because it always brought up the perfect weather in our hometown: warm and dry and bright. Dad got to name the four boys, so mom got to name me—not after an evangelist, but after the month she met dad. It was the beauty of June—the month—that made suffering through Januarys and Februarys seem meaningful.

"What about applying at another shop?" I said. "Joining a union? Running for office? Your personality is suited for leadership—Dad always said so."

He told me I should be glad that he wasn't hawking painkillers like the rest of his friends, that unions didn't give a fuck about anything but their pensions, that politics was an even bigger racket than the Church. All about money, everything about money. "What—you think there's gonna be a revolution? That we're going to drag the rich people out into the fucking street? Politics are nonsense."

"Money pays the mortgage," I said. I poured more whiskey in the spoon; he winced as he parted his lips. "It pays for *this* painkiller."

"You don't understand, June. Thanks for the support, but you don't understand."

. . .

When Father's Day came, the boys wanted to do something special for the next home game: a visual tribute to our dad, green letters on individual sheets of white. Mark wanted me to paint the signs—his hands were too bloody, the scrapes wouldn't heal. Mark was a drifter, the family fuckup who never got his wake-up call, even when dad passed and mom hit the bottle. He was the first one our mom would ask about when I visited her in her filthy apartment, chattering through shaky hands and menthol smoke about his priors and con jobs, still pulling for him to not wind up grizzled and bitter like her.

"But June," Mark said, "it's like I'm actually a part of something now."

"What about being part of the workforce?" I asked as I painted cardboard slabs with **ALWAYS IN OUR HEARTS** in green paint. "What about being part of the universal church? You're the smart one, you know. Dad always said so."

"The service economy is bullshit. No dignity in the work anymore."

"I'm serving you, Mark!"

"You don't understand, June. I love you to death, but you don't understand."

I pulled back my hair and started cleaning the organ at St. James Church. I'd asked Father Berlinski for more work around the church, told him that Matt was still out of work and that money was getting tight. He knew I'd only gotten through three semesters at Oakland Community College before dad passed, knew about our mom's problems, my brothers.

"Those boys, dear," he said. "That's your life now."

So, he called in a favor from the archdiocese for some extra funds to pay me for cleaning the organ pipes.

I told them I would pray for them at Mass, and they said *thanks, but no thanks.*

. . .

Dad was the real Catholic—his dad brought the faith with him from Warsaw when he came over to work on the line for Ford, back when you could. Dad always maintained it was his sincerest wish—the wish he died with when lung cancer took him—that we stay together in the Church, that he'd always be with us there. But mom's faith died with him. Her favorite excuse for drinking was the desire to *hurry this bullshit up* so she could get back together with him. The four boys felt abandoned in their own ways, but as I moved from the organ to the chapel, Windexing the stained glass, I thought about how all the chaos around me—from the manufacturing jobs disappearing, dad's death, mom's addiction, my brothers' descent into cultish violence—had reaffirmed my faith. Like the Holy Mother after the Deposition staring into the blank face of her only child, born to die, of her face on Michelangelo's *Pietà*. I prayed for all of them after washing the dust from my hair in the janitor's closet. Then I walked home to more drinking, more chanting, more tall tales of physical transcendence through obliteration.

After they set off Roman candles at the Jackson team's home stadium on the Fourth of July, Luke came back from the library with scribbled notes from YouTube videos (there was no computer at the house, and we communicated through prepaid Nokias from the local Kroger) about the *proper firms* of England. He asked me to drive him to Kinkos and print flyers so he could canvass the neighborhood for new believers. Luke had dropped out of the seminary when dad passed, saying that no god would turn his back on our family the way his had. Luke said he wanted to transition the group away from violence into something that more resembled a congregation that would unite team and supporters in song. This unity through exultation would mute the savagery, help everyone appreciate small moments of joy. That was the real tragedy of life, he said. Not that it ended, but that it went on too long—years and years without end. Here Luke was, decked in green robes, hitting the pavement with his gospel, his Word.

"I only said that 'cause I lost my faith, June. I was grieving. I still am."

I told him that I was, too; that grief is not something to experience alone. I told him that there was a God for hamstrung existences like ours, that it was easy to feel like the Rapture had come and we'd been left behind.

"You don't understand, June. I admire your faith, but you don't understand."

Deep down, if I really dug into my faith, I knew there was a very good chance it might be a lie. But during communion, during that moment I was convinced I was consuming the physical host of unconditional love, I didn't care. That's the power of ritual: like drinking round after round until your nose runs and your stomach warps, like chanting show tunes with ironic, cynical lyrics, like being punched so hard your teeth fall out. It's ritual that stops us from going crazy about how different our lives could have been.

Johnny, baby Johnny, always seemed cautious, thoughtful, sensitive. He landscaped around the neighborhood and put his money in the three mason jars labeled **FOOD, UTLITIES, CLOTHES**. But when he got dumped by his girlfriend, some mousey west side bitch who thought working-class life was beneath her, he lost himself in the team, traveling to Flint and Saginaw and Battle Creek, beating up other soccer gangs with names like the Billy Durants, the SagNasties, the Cereal Killers. In the dog days of August, he came back from Muskegon with two black eyes. The other boys serenaded him with early Motown-era Stevie Wonder songs as I sealed his cuts with rubber cement.

"Keep it down, you'll wake the neighbors," I said.

They started singing "My Cherie Amour," the song dad used to sing to mom on summer nights, the song she mumbled in her sleep after marathon benders. "Don't ruin it for me," I mourned.

One of them sang, "*La la laaa, laaa la la.*"

One of them said, "You don't understand, June. You'll never understand."

• • •

When I picked mom up and brought her over for the family Labor Day picnic of pasta salad and bologna sandwiches, she hugged the boys weakly and they all took turns laughing and crying over their favorite dad stories as I scrubbed dishes and collected cans. Late in the evening, when she had had too many beers, she said she didn't remember the boys being so close, so happy, so full of purpose. And I pay for it all, I muttered. The whole damn thing. As she slept it off in my bed later, the boys told me I had to come to the final game—that there'd be a spectacle I just *had* to see.

I went to that game. I sat high up in the home bleachers, looking across at the visitors' bleachers filled with drunk, howling kids from Bay City silhouetted against the rush hour traffic on Nine Mile Road. Beneath me, my brothers and a hundred other green-clad boys their age chanted some tasteless variant of "Consider Yourself" from *Oliver!*, like their authentic English counterparts do across the ocean. A cold September draft whistled through the aluminum bleachers, and I pulled my consignment store sweater tighter and thought about all those hats and gloves they'd need for the coming winter, what I was going to do for Christmas. After the other fans returned serve, the Acolytes sang a version of "For Once in My Life," arm in arm, passing flasks of whiskey. I closed my eyes, whispering "Salve Regina" as the goal nets rippled. Suddenly, I heard a rumble from their section. I heard my brothers yell in unison, "Now!" and a huge green banner unfurled from the top row. It read: **FOR JUNE, OUR HOLY MOTHER**. They broke into a rendition of "Hey Jude" with my name in the refrain.

I watched my brothers, their painted faces singing my name, eyes welling with tears. They sang and swayed, then unlocked their arms and beckoned me to join them.

I stood up and walked over to them. As they embraced me, the entire section roared.

All dad ever asked for was for the family to stay together, away from drugs and crime and selfish lovers—to hold on tight when the bottom fell out. Maybe the Acolytes were the answer to his prayers and mine, after all.

BEN

Constellations

Jimmy first comes to me with bad breath—it's sour and damp as he sways side to side down my street on a hot summer night. He embraces me awkwardly before reaching into his shorts and pulling out a pint of Mohawk Whiskey.

"This stuff tastes awful," he says, "but it makes you feel really numb. Like nothing can hurt you."

He offers me the bottle, but I turn away, saying that if my parents ever find out I've been drinking I'd be grounded for the rest of my life. We are both starting high school at Ferndale, and I don't want to risk anything.

"There's gotta be a little risk," he says. "Otherwise, it's no fun."

We walk down East Nine Mile to I-75 and put our legs over the railing and watch the cars, white lights driving into Detroit, red lights hurtling away toward the suburbs.

We talk about how we met in the exhaust stink of the Woodward Dream Cruise. Our dads, friends from work at the fabricating shop on Hilton Road, had both entered their classic cars in the Ferndale contest. We shared stories about growing up, about grade school, about our neighborhood that he found so claustrophobic and I found so limiting. He told me about drinking Pop Rocks with Surge, making out with older girls, going for joyrides in his neighbors' cars. Back then, Jimmy told me that he didn't do any of it to impress people or get even with his parents. He wanted something else, something he could only articulate when he shared his thoughts with someone who actually listened. As we packed up in the twilight, he shouted over the roaring engines and screeching tires that it was like we had known each other for a long, long time.

Now, he takes one last swig and tosses the bottle over the railing. "What do you want, Ben?"

"To be happy. Just to be happy, that's all."

"What would make you happy?"

It doesn't take me long to think. "I want to meet a nice girl . . . one who likes me for who I am. I want a house farther north on Woodward, not down here, because I want to be able to see the stars at night." I hesitate. "And I want a kid."

He hawks spitballs at the cars under our feet. "That's all? Seriously?"

"Why? What do you want?"

He stares across the freeway, at the cars cutting each other off, the semis on their way up north. "I wanna be free."

I laugh at him, his ignorance, his arrogance, the simplicity of an answer I know can't be realized. "You can't really be free."

"Course I can. I just can't have anything attached to me."

I look up at the night sky and try to make out the stars. It's almost impossible from the streetlights, the exhaust.

High school brings progress reports every quarter, which means I see Jimmy sporadically, between his zero hours and suspensions and curfews. He routinely fails all of his classes, which he never attends, and when he does, he's so disruptive that he's sent to the principal's office. Every teacher says Jimmy is a smart kid, extremely so, but that he's too undisciplined, reckless, that he has no respect for anyone.

I ask him all the time: "Why do you do it? Why steal hubcaps with all the dropouts outside of school, drink in the bathrooms, hook up with the bad upper-class girls in their beat-up domestic cars in the parking lot?"

He tilts his head back, smiles, slaps his legs. "I mean it's boring after a while, man. They do the same fucking things constantly . . . they're not going to go anywhere ten miles out of town their whole life. But shit, can you really keep your eyes open more than ten minutes in those boring-ass classes? I mean, honestly! It's like the goddamn shop our dads work at, getting barked at by the boss all day, every day, Jesus. That's no way to live." Then he pauses, stares at me, earnestly. "But more and more keep closing—the shops, I mean. My dad says stuff about outsourcing, whatever that is."

My dad says the same thing, that I won't have the chance to make a living the way he has, have a life of overtime pay and beer league softball at Martin Road Park, of summer weekends on Lake Huron. That I need to get my shit together and get into a decent college, get a job where I don't have to use my hands.

After sophomore year my parents start telling me that I shouldn't hang around Jimmy; that he's bad news, a fuckup. But he's still my best friend, and every time I talk to him I'm filled with a kind of passion I can't find at school, at home, anywhere. His world is exotic to me. Jimmy is on these adventures, and I'm happy that when he comes back from them, I'm the first person he tells them to.

By the time spring of senior year rolls around and I'm accepted to Michigan State, Jimmy's been out of school for two years. He works afternoons at Dynamic and spends most of his time at the bars around town with his fake ID, carousing with the bikers and pool sharks and single mothers from the dying blue-collar class in our corner of Ferndale. On graduation night he gets drunk at Kady's Bar on Nine Mile—they let all the graduates in after the all-night party at the high school—on bottles of Budweiser and Jameson. He calls me from their pay phone to walk him home.

We trace the same path we had four years earlier, the night air heavy with the bloom of late May—thick pollen cutting through the engine fumes and whistles from the train yard. We walk past shuttered shops and factories and body shops, reminding each other that our dads were our age all those years ago when they walked into those places, diplomas in hand, to start their working lives. Jimmy laughs, says, "Fuck 'em," then regales me with tales of late nights clouded with drink. I realize that even though I don't want to live like Jimmy, our personalities give balance to our friendship—that in some strange way, each of us needs the other. When we reach the I-75 overpass, he spits at the cars and puts a hand on my shoulder.

"I'm not just saying this 'cause I'm drunk, Benny. Our friendship is something that sustains me. I want to live a selfish life that will surround me with selfish people. It just goes with the territory. But you're an antidote for that. Someone who listens, understands. You're the only person I can communicate with. I don't know which one of us is gonna be right—probably me, just sayin'—but I'm gonna need you to be there for me."

"If you say so."

"Anyway," he looks up at the sky, "I'm glad you're getting out of here. Think I am, too."

"Send me a postcard," I say. "And don't do anything dumb."

He smiles. "I'll do my best."

I don't know it then, but after that night I will see Jimmy only three times over the next ten years.

Then Jimmy comes to me with joints, with cigar wrappers and glass bowls and giant bongs. He rides up to East Lansing in early November of my sophomore year in a hot Japanese sedan to sleep on the floor of my dorm room.

"I'm living in downtown Detroit," he says, lighting a joint. "I love the danger, Ben, the feeling of impending violence, crime. I'm dealing a pretty good amount down there, and I think I'm pretty good at it—I'm the only one with the stones to walk into the houses in Brightmoor and Highland Park where the weight is and bring it back to the Cass Corridor to break up and sell to the Wayne State students, the trust fund bohos, the high-strung white collars at GM and Quicken Loans and DTE." He fills the chamber of a bong with weed until it overflows, coughing out huge, thick clouds. "It's weird, man—everyone is in awe of me. It just feels amazing to be high all day, to sleep with whomever I want . . . to live the life I'm living. Everyone tells me I'm fearless," he rolls another joint filled with a strain that has a hip-hop nickname, "but that isn't quite true, not exactly."

"Why not?" I notice his languid movements, the redness of his eyes.

"I'm afraid of being happy, I guess." The room vibrates around us. "I figure if I'm happy I'll just settle in around Ferndale—job, mortgage, beer leagues." All I can do is nod my head and tap my foot to the White Stripes album Jimmy is blasting from my speakers. "But I guess when I'm high on this shit all day, I don't think about it."

He puffs the joint and holds his breath, the smoke circling his lungs and leaking out his nose. "I try to tell this to the people I'm with down there but all they can say is *stop thinking about it* or *chill the fuck out* or *you're harshing my vibes*." He takes another drag. "That's why I need a new scene, man. I shouldn't have to haul all the way up here to have a conversation with someone with a head on their shoulders, you know?"

"Where would you go?"

He shakes his head and watches some drunk freshmen stumble back to the dorms. "Somewhere I don't feel like I'm suffocating."

After an hour Jimmy says he's starving, so I take him to Menna's on Grand River and he orders fifty dollars' worth of food for us, pulling out a thick wad of rolled money. We sit back in a booth and Jimmy asks me how the semester is going. I tell him I spend a lot of time in the library and am on course to get a 4.0. I've made some friends in my dorm and we play Frisbee by the Red Cedar River, go to the football games on Saturdays. I feel embarrassed—my life seems so drab in comparison.

"What about the girls?" he asks.

I tell him about drunken makeouts I can barely remember, that in truth I don't like drinking or the hookup culture on campus, but that there's a girl in one of my lectures who always sits in the back corner, who seems shy and, to me, frighteningly pretty.

"It's like I'm scared of her," I say through mouthfuls of meat and cheese. "It's hard to explain."

He laughs and kicks me under the table. "Welcome to being in love!"

"I don't think . . ."

"Yeah, man, that's how that shit works. One day you're going through the motions, the routine, and you see someone and your stomach feels heavy and you get scared. That's how it all starts."

"It feels . . . bad?"

"Not bad, just, you know, intimidating?"

This realization courses through my body and I feel exhilarated. I ask Jimmy if he's ever been in love.

"Are you serious? Of course I have! But that kind of thing is too addicting, if you ask me. I don't want to mess with it. Besides, everyone

I know who falls in love pairs off and becomes lame. They totally, like, forfeit themselves. They compromise. Not for me."

When we finish, we walk around the bars on Abbott, Jimmy shaking his head and telling me what a waste of time it was being part of the drinking culture.

"You're a lucky kid, you know that?" Jimmy says.

"How do you figure?"

"You're not one of those people."

"What do you mean?"

"You think you're boring, man, and I'm telling you that all that . . ." he motions to the crowd of frat boys getting in fights, their sorority dates sharing cigarettes and checking their phones. "All that. Those people. That's boring. Trust me."

Back at my dorm, Jimmy smokes another joint on the front steps. We look up and watch the stars, which throb luminously in the cold night air.

The next morning, Jimmy is gone. He leaves a note saying he has some people to meet around campus, that he has to execute the "business" side of the trip, but that he misses me, every day, and that I am as close to a brother as he'll ever have. I notice a *PS* near the bottom with a crudely scribbled note: *Go talk to that girl.*

And I do.

Her name is Claire.

That day I walk with her to her art class and she shows me her work—contemporary triptychs in the style of the Flemish Primitives. She paints in tempera, making the rich colors of factory workers' clothes pop in her favorite piece—left panel family life, center panel factory work, right panel Sunday Mass.

"If you really start looking at the essence of things," she says, pulling her brown hair behind her ears, "of blades of grass, leaves of autumnal trees, individual drops of rain—paintings can compose themselves."

I ask her what she means, trying to avoid her eyes.

"I don't believe in God, or at least a human God, but do I believe that everything we perceive has an essence, and if you concentrate and reject all the pretentiousness and falsity of the world you can capture what really matters: the distilled passion of *this* life and how essential work is." Afterward, when I walk her back to her dorm, she asks what my passion is and why I can't stop smiling. We kiss.

The next day we skip class and drive to her parents' house in Berkley, a few miles north on Woodward from where I grew up. She shows me her high school paintings, laughs at the ones she calls "juvenile." We drive down Woodward and turn off at Nine Mile, and I walk her around my old neighborhood, telling her stories about high school, about Jimmy. We get on I-75 and drive into Detroit to visit the DIA. In the medieval wing, she shows me the Flemish paintings that inspire her, spending an hour in front of Bruegel's *The Wedding Dance*, picking out the range of emotion painted on every face. We leave to eat Coney Island hotdogs at Lafayette and take the elevator to the top floor of the Renaissance Center and watch the sunset splash color on the river, talking about our dreams: hers to be a great American painter, mine to surround myself with people I care about. She tells me she envies my simplicity. I tell her I envy her passion.

"Why?" she asks, watching the freighters float below us. "You become a slave to your own ambition."

"I don't see it like that. Not everyone has the tools to construct their own meaning. You're a lot like Jimmy in that way." I lean against the glass. "I like being close to it, I guess."

Claire holds my hand.

We spend the next week together, breathless and lost in an unbroken conversation, and when we make love for the first time, we stare into each other's eyes. As she breathes deeply, I think she's looking for my essence, and when I hold her afterward, I silently pray that she found mine—whatever it is—and that it's enough for her. A month later, walking hand in hand in the shadow of Beaumont Tower, she stops, turns me around, and says, "I love you."

Then Jimmy comes to me with bulging eyes and a bloody nose, sniffing and twitching. He bangs on the window of my rental bungalow in Royal Oak, throws little pieces of gravel so hard they crack the glass. I let him in, and he asks for a drink. I tell him what time it is, how I need to be in

Birmingham at nine for work, and he tells me to suck it up, goes straight for the liquor cabinet and pours himself a whiskey.

"Sorry," he says. "I just need to come down a little bit." He taps his feet furiously and runs his hands through his greasy hair.

After a few minutes, he stops shaking. "It's wonderful to see you, just wonderful. Desperately sorry for not returning your calls—I lose cell phones every week, you know?" He looks around the kitchen. "How long's it been, anyway?"

"Four years, more or less."

"Time flies, Benny. Fuck, four years." He looks tired suddenly. I change the subject.

"I kept all the postcards you sent me."

"No shit? Lemme see."

I walk to the living room and pull them from a drawer. They recount the entirety of Jimmy's journey, and as I flip through them, I glance worryingly at him, blinking and laughing awkwardly in his chair.

After a few more drinks he launches into a story. "When I left Detroit I sort of bounced around the west for a while, living off the sale of the trunk full of weed I brought with me, a goodbye present from my 'business partners.' I remember the rainy days in Olympia, where you can see three rainbows strung across the waters of the Puget Sound; the noise the wind makes as it blows across the Sandhills in Nebraska, like the collective howl of fallen angels. The only thing I saw that's impossible to describe in our language was the sun rising in the Arizona desert."

He looks thinner under the overhead lights. "Sounds beautiful."

"You have no idea, Benny. Anyways, I settled in Los Angeles and became an extra, working just enough to pay for my room in Los Feliz. I spent most of my free time—which I had a great deal of, finally—commiserating with vagrants on Venice Beach, sleeping with Midwestern teenagers holed up in the Valley waiting for their callbacks and partying in the Hills with my casting agent, and it was at one of those parties that I first tried cocaine."

"Cocaine?" I ask.

"I never did it in Detroit because by the time it got that far north it was cut with Novocaine and baby powder so much it barely kicked. That's what the coke dealers said, anyway—that Detroit coke is shit coke. But I had always heard about the Hollywood stuff, and Jesus Christ, it is something else."

"I wouldn't know either way."

"It feels like someone wrapping you up in the softest blanket you could imagine and whispering things that made you smile ear to ear. It makes you feel invincible. If you bottled the emotion you feel right after you come, it would almost approach the way it makes you feel."

I think about telling him to be careful, to take it easy, but before I can, he says, "Enough about me. What's new with you, Benny?"

After collecting my thoughts, I tell him things are busy. I had graduated with a degree in financial planning so I could help people finance their dreams, and I tell him that my internship at Merrill Lynch in Birmingham has turned into a full-time position. Claire's busy, too—she's at Cranbrook getting her MFA in painting. We stay up late most nights in our attic, me researching the bond market for one of our mutual funds, Claire at the window, painting the changing sky for her latest piece: a look at life before, during, and after industry in Detroit in the fore-, middle-, and backgrounds. I tell him that I'm engaged—the wedding scheduled for the fall of next year.

"This goes without saying," I smile, concern about Jimmy's haggard appearance dissipating into familiarity, "but will you be the best man?"

"It would be an honor, Benny. Are you kidding me, of fucking course!"

We embrace. I ask him if he wants anything to eat and he shakes his head no but asks if he can use the bathroom. He leaves and returns a few minutes later, eyes bulging, nostrils flared.

"So where to now?" I ask.

"Back west. Think I'm gonna do the Hollywood thing until it gets boring. Who knows, you might see me on the big screen one day—in a real role, I mean."

At the top of the stairs, Claire pokes her head down. I try to wave her back upstairs, but Jimmy's seen her, walks over and extends his hand.

"I've heard so much about you," he says.

Claire smiles, nervously watching Jimmy grind his teeth. "Good things, I hope."

"Only the best. What a catch, Benny! You know, I'm sorta the reason you two got together."

Claire looks at me. "Is that so?"

"He was too nervous to talk to you. Had to give him a pep talk." He checks his watch and clears his nose. "Gotta go, you two—I have a meeting in Bloomfield Hills. A producer, wants me to go over some lines with him."

He gives us both a shaky hug and writes down his casting agent's address—the best place, he says, to send the save the date. After he leaves, Claire asks me how Jimmy is. I say fine, I think he is, maybe, and that she should have come down earlier. She shakes her head and tells me she wishes my best friend could be a stable part of my life, ours.

Claire isn't bothered by my lack of friends—we're both solitary people and we keep each other's solitude—but she's always disturbed by the stories I tell about Jimmy, disturbed that I tell his saga of personal annihilation with gusto, something she says approaches admiration, if not envy. I laugh it off and tell her that everyone grows up needing someone to look up to, trust, respect—someone that when they are young and weak and intimidated by cruel children and authoritarian adults, they need in a very primal way. When she asks if I think he needs help, I shake my head and say that Jimmy can take care of himself, that he did when he was fourteen, that he can now, and that he always will.

But secretly, I worry. In the next few months, Jimmy's postcards arrive more and more infrequently, the handwriting becoming nearly illegible. As she moves through her program, Claire begins stripping her work down to reflect what's left of industry in our hometowns, painting only in shades of black, white, and gray, experimenting with textures, the compositions holding increasingly abstract narratives. She tells me about blurring the colors we view as extremes, how the reality of their essence holds secrets more complex than mere surface value. I find myself thinking of Jimmy as we lie in our bed on Sunday afternoons listening to live opera broadcasts from Toronto on our transistor radio. In the triangulation of my life, I find myself as the base star that props up two others that shine fiercely and burn brightly but without which the cosmic pattern loses its connection, its meaning.

It isn't perfect, of course. Claire wins prizes, grants, the MFA faculty fawning over her evolving technique. But she can't secure a lucrative solo exhibition at the trendy Birmingham galleries, and so can't take the next step.

"It figures," she says one night after another rejection email. "All those Birmingham art collectors are scions of industrial ownership. I'm sure they don't want to see the way of life they've helped destroy hanging in their living rooms."

Our living room is filled with Claire's interpretations of our travels together: hiking the Sleeping Bear Dunes, eating popcorn in the back row of the Redford Theatre, and kayaking the Red Cedar, where, after fleeing back to campus in a driving rainstorm, I proposed.

In the months leading up to the wedding, the postcards stop coming altogether, and in my anxiety I begin to grow into Claire, noticing the way her lips curl when she's frustrated, how her eyes widen when something visual moves her. In August, after my dad's old shop Dynamic Fabricating finally closes, we drive over so Claire can paint the façade, with its graffiti and broken windows. When she looks back at me it's like I'm seeing her for the first time: the blonde streaks in her hair, the blue in her eyes, the intensity that burns in the features of people possessed by something that transcends the mundane. I feel something inside me shift permanently, and realize that as long as I have Claire and Claire's love, I will be happy.

When Jimmy doesn't show up for the ceremony, I pretend not to notice. My father does the honors next to me, and as I look into Claire's eyes, I know that I have become impossibly close with someone who sustains me, who needs my help to communicate something essential.

Then Jimmy comes to me with holes in his arms, gray skin, and yellow eyes. He forces the door open with a broken screwdriver and lies on the floor moaning until I come downstairs.

I barely recognize him. For a moment I think he's been shot and rush to his side, pulling my phone out to dial 911. I wrap him in a blanket to assuage his shivering, sit him upright in the kitchen, and made him a cup of black coffee.

It takes a while for the caffeine to kick in. When it does, he says, "I already went to your parents' house to find out where you lived. They look good."

"So," I say, choking back tears. "How's the movie star life?"

"Oh, that. I got tired of Hollywood. After a few years everyone turns plastic and loses their soul. I got tired of playing the same role in the background, and even so, I don't understand why we idolize actors and actresses—they're just a bunch of selfish, insecure pricks.

"Most of all," he says, "I got sick of the weather, the climate—it's the same goddamn day every day. I don't care if it's nice—it gets to you, trust me. After a while, nothing felt real."

I search for something to say. "And then?"

"I sold my car and bought a train ticket to El Paso and found a job as a ranch hand. I thought it'd be romantic, I guess. I got reacquainted with work by putting in sixteen-hour days, longer days than the migrant workers, reacquainted with culture by reading everything I could find." He takes a deep breath, then coughs violently. "One night I was in the library looking for a copy of *The Sun Also Rises* when I saw someone's shadow slumped in the corner, a silhouetted arm rising and falling. Approaching from the side, I recognized someone I worked with, a belt hanging from his mouth.

"He asked me if I wanted a hit, and, I dunno, I must have been bored or something, so he pulled out a lighter and a spoon and tied me up, and oooohhhh, Benny . . ." His eyes roll back into his head and a smile blooms slowly over his bearded face.

"It gets fuzzy after that, honestly. It started slowly, then grew. Soon I was up all night doing it, then all day. Didn't take long for the rancher to kick me out. Then I bummed around El Paso, hanging with other junkies, finally understanding the Stones' *Exile on Main St.* After I ran out of money and pawned the few things I could lift from electronics stores, I went in on a drug deal where I carried a brick up to New York. I took the money from that and moved to Brooklyn to be a junkie full-time. It's crazy how the stuff can get you, but honestly you just have to let it, you have to give into it the way people give in to Jesus, give in to capitalism, let it consume you, all of you. But Brooklyn was tough—everything was gentrifying too fast; I'd have to move to the squatters lounge every three months or so. The advance was rampant, unrelenting."

"What are you referring to?" I ask.

"Huh?"

"The advance. The unrelenting advance."

His eyes glaze over and he rolls back his head. "After a year I moved to Jersey City. I don't remember anything after that." He coughs again. "Listen to me go on and on. What about you, Benny?"

Through damp eyes and clenched fists, I tell him about my promotion, which meant that Claire and I could afford to move to Birmingham, which we did, and that Claire is pregnant. I tell him that after Claire finished her MFA, she began teaching art at the Roeper School within walking distance of our new house, and that it made her very happy. I tell him that planning for our child—a girl we had already christened Jane—has taken up most of our time recently, and how I feel that having her would fulfill my dreams, complete my life.

I don't tell him about the night I heard crashing sounds coming from the garage, that I walked out and opened the door and found Claire in the dark. I turned on the light and saw holes punched in her paintings—the canvasses ripped, the frames smashed—her entire inventory wetly spotted with white and black paint. When I moved toward her, she turned her back on me.

"I'm never going to make it," she said.

"You already have, haven't you? Haven't you created something you're passionate about, something timeless?"

"No. I'll never be an *artist*, Ben."

"I don't understand the difference."

She reached under a wooden bench and pulled out two paintings. One was the first triptych she showed me when we were sophomores at

Michigan State, the other her most recent: the frame of a hollowed factory composed of different textures of black paint.

"I've been thinking about a way to tell you this for a while now." She stood and cleared her throat. "Ben, I know you want a child. You told me on our first date. And if we have a child, I won't be able to paint. I'm afraid all of my time will be consumed by it . . . this sacrificing of yourself, your passion, so someone else might be happy. And my work . . . it will suffer."

Words held themselves in her mouth as I arched my back and held my breath.

"I guess I thought I would have been there by now; the place I've always wanted to be. I never prepared for the idea that I might never make it. And if this is it and I never do, then everything about my life will need to change. I won't want anything around to remind me of my failure." She reached out and held my hand. "I'm sorry, Ben. I don't expect you to understand. I think I might need to be alone. For a while, at least."

My stomach curdled; my jaw tightened. I steadied myself, walked out, and shut the door behind me. Back in the house, I walked up to our bedroom. Sitting on the bed I had shared for seven years with the woman I knew to be my great love, I realized she was right, and I could think only of Jimmy out west, rolling the hills and valleys with elegant terror.

I grabbed my car keys and walked to the front door, playing with the knob in my hand. I had a choice to make—to leave Claire to her passion, find Jimmy and have him help me find mine, or lie down on our bed and wait for her to come back inside.

I went back to bed.

She came inside the next morning, burrowed into my arms, and said she was sorry. Three weeks later, after another rejection from a gallery in Charlevoix, she went off the pill.

"I don't think this is like the other times, Jimmy. You look like you're dying."

"I'm not going to die. Nothing can kill me if I don't think it will, remember?"

Now I see the flame in his eyes again, briefly, the smoldering violence that exists inside him, the unquenchable thirst for a life that I can never interpret, a thirst that tosses him from shore to shore, a thirst that can be sated only briefly by dulling it, relegating it in all its intensity to the margins, and only there can he breathe. Jimmy chokes on life, on this world, and in his sickness now I see the bravery and suffering of the "free," now shackled and pathetic, reduced like all things to baseness.

"You're addicted," I say.

"I'm not addicted. Addiction is a word tossed around by the weak . . . the fearful. Everything I put into my body I can control. You've known me long enough . . ."

"Do you have any idea how you make the people who love you feel? Does it ever cross your mind?"

He sneers and turns away. "I never wanted people to love me, but sure."

"Then why do you do it?"

He looks at me, at my white shirt with a buttoned collar and Brooks Brothers tie, at my shined black shoes, past me to the living room with the big TV where Claire normally watches her PBS documentaries on the great American painters, and I think I can see his eyes move up the stairs to the guest room that will become my daughter's once Claire picks out the color, once Claire picks out the crib.

Then he looks back at me. "Look, I've never asked you for much, have I?"

"I can help you, Jimmy."

"Great. I just need fifty bucks, Benny. Fifty bucks to last me until I can get back on my feet."

I shake my head. "Not like that."

He swallows. "Sorry. It was stupid to ask." He finishes his coffee, stands up, and embraces me, weakly. "I'll see you soon, Benny."

When he leaves, I lock the front door, then the back door, then walk around the house closing the windows, drawing the blinds. When I'm finished and am sure there is no way Jimmy can get in the house, I sit down in the vestibule and weep.

. . .

Every time my phone rings, I fear the worst. I know Jimmy's parents will be on the other end, trying to steady themselves; old acquaintances from our neighborhood and high school, giving hollow condolences; strangers who met Jimmy throughout his life telling me how sorry they are, but that deep down with all the anger, there must be a measure of relief.

I don't want to hear any of it. I'm not ready for Jimmy to be dead. I readily volunteer to run errands for a pregnant Claire, crying from trip to trip.

On Jane's first birthday, I receive a letter in the mail. The return address is "Lighthouse, May's Landing, New Jersey." It reads:

> I called home a few weeks ago and my dad told me about your daughter, that today, or the day you should be getting this, I hope, she celebrates her first anniversary on this earth. I want to let you know that I'm "drying out," as they say, and when I do I want to come home and, well, join "society," I guess. I'm sorry for all the pain and stress I may have caused you—this is the Ninth Step, as we in the recovery community call it—but I feel that my affair with the rougher side of life is over. Just like with booze back in our high school days, I am bored with it. My best to Claire and little Jane—tell her Uncle Jimmy sends his best.

I carry the letter out into the backyard. Claire is bouncing Jane in her arms. The colors of Jane's watercolor birthday dress catch in the light— I'd rocked her gently when Claire painted it in brilliant splashes of reds, blues, yellows. Jane smiles and reaches for the letter. I hand it to Claire and hold Jane in my arms.

So now Jimmy comes to me drinking Maxwell House from a Salvation Army mug, chain-smoking cheap cigarettes on my porch, showing me his pocket calendar of crossed out days. He shakes and giggles and lifts up his shirt, showing me the running tally he's tattooing on himself—he can't get enough of the pain of the needle—crisscrossing his chest. He tells me about the weekly meetings, the support groups. He lives in a halfway house in Waterford and works as a line cook at a chain restaurant. He's taken up biking—he bikes twelve miles to Birmingham to see me, twelve miles back, as fast as he can—and talks about how stupid he was for such a long time, how many mistakes he's made.

Only this time it's me who says, *but Jimmy you've seen the whole country, Jimmy you've met so many people, Jimmy you've lived my life for me . . .*

And he just slaps his legs and lifts his head up and smiles, like he always has. He always brings presents for Jane—usually candy, which Claire and I won't let her have—and spends hours on the front lawn with her, building forts with cardboard boxes and playing tag. He stays late into the night when he visits—fifteen years of wasted energy is his excuse—and before he leaves we stand on my front lawn in the quiet darkness to say our goodbyes.

Maybe it's because his years on the road have fried his short-term memory, but the conversations are always the same.

"We're lucky, aren't we Benny?"

"If you say so."

"How's Claire?"

"She's happy."

"And you?"

"I'm happy."

"That was one thing I could never tell you." He takes a sip of coffee. "Until now, I guess." He stands up and stretches, and I see all the scars on his body, the pockmarks on his face, the accumulation of a dangerous life. "I was never happy, and I never wanted to be. I never liked what happiness did to other people . . . how it killed them . . ."

Then he turns and faces me.

"But I was wrong. Must've been the drugs."

When he leaves, I walk upstairs to Jane's room and make sure she's asleep. I turn off her nightlight and the ceiling bursts into a sky full of fluorescent yellow stars. Claire and I made it the night she found out she was pregnant; we walked down Old Woodward kissing and laughing until we got to CVS and bought packs and packs of them, and when we got home we went upstairs to the guest bedroom and made love on the hardwood floor and opened the window to look at the stars through the trees. It was late summer and we could see the constellations—Lyra, Sagittarius, almost all of them. We took the stars out of the bag and I held Claire up to the ceiling and we made our own sky, star for star, all the constellations to catch our child's dreams.

I marvel at the fake sky I made for my daughter, my dreams hanging there with hers, strung up in a limitless hope for a passion I have never found, a hope that is now extinguished in my wife and in my best friend.

My daughter sleeps as I look up at the constellations, and I wonder if they will always be that bright.

GINA

Was It Good for You?

"I've never done this before."

"That's sweet." I laugh at the voice. "What do you like, sweetheart?" I don't look at the pictures of the people I see in the bottom corner of my screen. They're my clients, and I don't want to attach a face to the things I do for them, the things I make them do.

"Um, well . . . do you have any, any things?"

I reach over to the bedside table between the burning candles and grab my favorite toy, waving it slowly in front of the camera.

"That's fine. That should work."

I imagine the other eyes, dry from staying open, stretched, aching in anticipation as I click and start the timer. "How do you like it?" This is the part in the dialogue where I know how much I'm going to make. It's where they show their cards—what makes them tick, squirm, explode.

"No one's asked me that before . . ."

"Join the club." Nervous erotic energy. Power shifting. I begin. "Does this turn you on?"

When my dad left, he told me, "You're a pretty girl, Gina, a lot of girls ain't. Boys like pretty girls, you know that, right?"

I nodded and stared at my pretty reflection in the hallway mirror and thought about my mom at my age, if her dad had ever said this to her, how she wound up with a man like my dad.

"You can make a lot of money, sweetheart. In this country, in this town you can make a living off your looks."

Sometimes, when I refresh my page and minimize the window in the corner of my screen, I imagine my dad staring through the other lens, taste his shame the moment I take off my bra and he sees how pretty I've become.

• • •

When it's over I'm flushed, sweating, my windows fogged. The radiator hums and exhales its murky heat. I like this job if only because it keeps me warm during the bleak midwinters in Detroit.

"Can I ask you something?"

I forgot to close the browser. "Sorry, sweetheart. I'm afraid I'm tapped out."

"No, I don't want you to do anything else . . . I'll keep paying you, if you'd like."

"Trouble with the wife?"

"Not exactly."

"What's your question?"

"Do you ever feel . . . feel like there's something wrong? Like you're not living the way you're supposed to? Like everything that's supposed to matter is a lie?"

I hesitate. "Yeah."

"My wife doesn't understand. She just thinks I'm bored with her."

"Come back same time next week. Let's see if we can't work something out."

"Wear something . . . wear something coarse."

I hear a click in the other room. It's faint, but I have perceptive senses—very perceptive.

I pull the covers up and close my laptop as Rose, my great aunt, opens my door, sticks her head in the room.

"Busy day?"

The *b* lilts like it's caught between her tongue and the top of her mouth. Must not have her hearing aids up.

"Very," I shout.

She cranes her neck to the right and fidgets with her lobe.

"Are you coming tonight, dear?"

She's always trying to get me to go to Mass with her. When she was a nurse, she used to go every night after she clocked out. I humor her sometimes; after all, she's putting me up. "I have plans."

"Next time?"

"Next time. I promise."

Other than Catholicism, Auntie Rose's favorite lecture is about me working—about how I need to get a job and save my money to get an education for a job that women like her could only dream about when they were my age. Then I have to tell her a lie (that I would never sell myself short), and then tell her a truth (that no one can get a job right now because there is no work to do).

"Don't get too far from the Word, sweetheart. You start chasing worldly things you'll wind up like your mother."

"Not that."

"Sorry?"

"I don't like things, Auntie Rose."

And every time I think *yeah, maybe I do like things, maybe I want them*, all I have to do is take John R out to Eight Mile to I-75 North and get off at Big Beaver. A few miles west and I'm at the Somerset Collection, which, for those not familiar, is Detroit's answer to the delicious material want of the urban centers that still have consumers. You know—Nordstrom and Neiman Marcus; Hugo Boss, Gucci, Versace. Disembodied wealth in all of its meaninglessness. Prices so absurd that I have to remind myself that they are just commodities made from base materials that someone has decided costs an amount of money so outrageous it makes me feel sick.

So, I do. It's a Wednesday afternoon and my windows are all fogged from the melting snow—the weather lady on WJR says it's forty-five degrees. Almost a record for January. It feels hotter, especially when I get out of my Cutlass Supreme and unwrap my scarf from around my neck. The valet boys—valet parking for a mall—watch my movement, first like wolves, then like puppies as I walk by and flick my keys away.

The crowd at Somerset during the day is the same: the women who married well and don't have to go through the indignity of work and the kids from Troy High, Athens, and private schools skipping class.

"Can I help you?"

I'm browsing the cashmere sweaters at Ralph Lauren and there's a tall, dark-haired sales associate next to me. "I'm looking for something . . . flattering."

"Flattering?" He's not sizing me up. His eyes stay on mine.

"I'm seeing someone later who likes rough material."

"A wool blend, cut short with a low hanging neck?"

"It won't be too itchy, will it?"

"Depends on the person."

"He's very . . . he's very particular."

"It'll be rough when he touches you."

"Oh, he won't be doing that. It's an . . . an online date."

"What's that supposed to mean?"

"It's . . . I do performance art. In front of a webcam." I wink.

"Oh," he says, face intimidated, then intrigued. "Where do you . . . perform?"

"Ferndale."

"With all the workers. How romantic."

"Yeah well, not too much work to do now, is there, smartass?"

"People made these clothes."

I turn the sweater inside out. "In fucking Burma."

"I'm Brad," he says.

"Have a good week?" I start the timer.

"Not really."

"What can I do to make you feel better?" I start to take off that itchy sweater from the mall and think briefly about Brad, about seeing him tomorrow.

"You don't have to . . ."

I reach for the toy he liked last week. "Clothes on this time?"

"No, I mean . . ." I hear breathing, a heavy sigh. "Can we just talk?"

"It's your money."

"I've been feeling . . . I dunno . . . depressed?"

"It's January. Everyone's depressed."

"No, I don't think it's that. It's, well . . . I lied, the last time we . . . it's my wife."

"Most of my clients have trouble with their wives."

"My wife is beautiful. She always has been. We've always had a great, um, we've always been compatible romantically. But lately she's been—she's been asking to use other things in bed, other objects?"

"And you feel threatened."

"Not at all. It was a few weeks ago. She took these things out of her closet, and while she was doing it, I looked over her shoulder and saw all of her . . . all of her stuff. Dresses, shoes, jewelry. And, I dunno. It's like I can't stop thinking about it. Like it's making me sick."

Cold air comes in through the window crack. Always colder at night.

"Does that make any sense?"

I can picture my mom out in California with her face-lift and tit job and tummy tuck. "Yeah."

The box feels stiff—too upright. The window door slides open, and I hear breathing coming from the other end.

"Bless me Father, for I have sinned."

Silence.

"Well, I haven't sinned, really. I don't believe in sin. Too much guilt."

Silence.

"My great aunt, she wants me to be more religious. It's important to her. She thinks without religion I'll be too materialistic."

Silence.

"And I oblige her because she's the only family I have left, and that's something I understand and respect, but I don't think you need to believe in something abstract to know right from wrong. Especially in a material world."

Nothing.

"Stuff like clothes, Father? Makes me sick to my stomach."

We're at breakfast afterward. Auntie Rose punctures her soft-boiled eggs with rye toast.

"Do you think Mom's happy?" I ask.

"Hmm?" She turns up her hearing aid.

"Happier in California?"

"I don't think anyone's happy there, sweetheart. Too much sun." Her rosary dips into her coffee. "Not like where your father's going."

"That's not very nice."

"Well, it's true."

"I don't think there's a hell, Auntie. Not literally, anyway."

"I'm sure, before he passes, that his whole life will flash before his eyes, and I'm sure he'll hear God ask him, 'Was it good? Was it worth it?'"

This is the part where she talks about sin, about work, about the relationship between them. I nod politely and pick at my oatmeal.

In front of the Louis Vuitton store on his break, Brad tells me how long he looked for work after his shop closed.

"I always found something erotic about it. You're using your hands to create something from raw materials. It's hot and noisy, smells like sawdust and metal . . . your vision is altered from the sweat and dust on your work goggles. You're making something using all of your senses."

"You go to school?"

"Yeah." We look at the purses, the shoes. "Philosophy at Detroit Mercy."

"Why don't you use it?"

"What, to make money?"

"Man's gotta eat."

"Why? So I can buy one of those?" He points at a $1,500 belt. I get that nauseous feeling and walk away.

We take the skywalk to the other side and I tell him about my job, my parents, how I wound up living with Auntie Rose.

"She's the only one of my grandma's siblings that's still alive." I stare at the watches on the models in front of Swarovski, crystals shimmering under fluorescent lights.

"Does she know what you do?"

"What do you think?"

"I think it's a little warm for January."

He talks for a while about his thesis on dialectical materialism as we linger in front of glass windows, sizing each other up. The skylight's streaked with melting snow.

"For me, it comes down to believing that our material world is not the authentic one," he says. "And since there is no God and thus no religion, the authentic world can only be created once producers and consumers become aware that material commodities are not authentic. Only relationships are."

"The fake world. Rockin' in the fake world."

"Do you ever . . . do you ever fake it?"

"We all fake it."

"What's that supposed to mean?"

"You're the philosophy major." The melting snow trickles faster. The roof like a river. "You figure it out."

"Do you ever get scared?"

The timer blinks. I reach to reset it, then lie down instead. "About what?"

"You know . . . about the whole thing? The big picture?"

I relax. "You mean about dying?"

"I dunno . . . I don't really consider this being alive."

"What do you look like?"

"You can't see?"

"I choose not to. I have that option."

"I'm pale, I'm soft, I'm rich, I'm scared . . ."

"Do you ever have doubt, Auntie?" We're sitting in front of the fireplace, burning synthetic logs.

"We all do, sweetheart."

"Then how can you have faith?"

"Because doubt isn't real, Gina." She puts her hand in mine, runs her wrinkled fingers over my smooth ones. "This is. This is almost real." She untangles our fingers and stares into the fire.

• • •

In the food court with Brad, I watch the thawing snow drip from the skylight, leaving icy patterns that smear my tiny reflection.

A sheepish boy keeps looking over from another table. He's real young—no more than sixteen, and the way he's looking at me, hot and scared, means he's probably seen my show. I wave him over.

"I'm a huge fan of yours," he says, eyes on the ground.

Brad looks at me, puzzled.

I lean in close to the kid. "That's the most fleeting experience you'll ever have."

"What?"

"All you'll have is the memory. And that leaves when you die."

He fidgets, stiffens, and walks away.

"None of them know anything about you," Brad says.

"That's part of the job."

Brad looks away. "Commodities like to touch each other, don't they?"

"Is that what I am? Is that all I am? A sex object?"

"Yeah."

"Why? Because I get paid for it? Because of how I look? Because of how I dress?"

He stares at the ground.

"Is that all I am to you? Is that all I am to anybody?"

Nothing.

"I'll tell you why I'm a fucking sex object. Because no matter how far my Auntie Rose made it, if you look pretty you're just a thing." I pick at my clothes. "A fucking sweater."

"I don't know if you can be a casualty of the material world if you consciously turn something rare and beautiful into a commodity."

I start to get angry, but when I look into his eyes all I can see is jealousy. I hold his hand.

"Hey, sweetheart," I say, starting the timer.

"Oh yeah, I forgot. I have to pay you."

"Free lunches, etc."

"Have you ever studied psychology?"

"A few courses at community college." I pull off my stockings. "Why?"

"I think you'd make a good therapist. You can stop there."

I leave them half-rolled, squeezing my calves.

"What do the other guys make you do?" he asks.

"Anything that gets them off."

"What about you?"

"You want to know what gets me off?"

"Yeah, if you want to put it that way. Sure."

"Both my parents left because they wanted . . . more. And you know, where I live, you can't really get a whole lot more. Might never be able to ever again. And the thought of that, of living not for relationships but for material makes me so anxious I could scream . . ."

There's a pause; I can hear the cars desperately rolling down I-75 to jobs no one wants to work but has to, to stores to buy their things, then back to a house like mine.

"But when I come there's nothing. For a little bit there's nothing. And the anticipation of leaving that world, this world . . ."

"Everything all right?"

"Yeah. Just a little wet."

"In nomine Patris, et Filii, et Spiritus Sancti."

Auntie Rose lights candles at an altar. Placed in the middle, bound by the wax of a thousand exhausted candles, is a picture of my Great Uncle Ron.

"Here, darling." She hands me a match. "I want you to do the last one."

I spark it and hold it up against the picture, searching for my uncle's faded face. Auntie Rose holds my hand.

"I'll see you soon, my love," she says. "The soul is immaterial."

I light the last candle.

"For dust thou art, and unto dust shalt thou return."

Wax drips onto my hand, burning and turning hard.

•   •   •

"Who decides what's sexy?" Brad asks. We're in California Pizza Kitchen sharing an appetizer. "Who decides what sex is—the gender, the act? Once you can commodify that you can start making money; you can turn an act of the senses, a natural act, into something material."

"The free market," I say. I look over at another table—a woman my age with bags from four different stores—and a shudder works its way up my spine.

"Why do you come here if it disgusts you?"

"To remind myself . . . to keep myself sane."

He fidgets in his seat, adjusts his merino cardigan. "Will you come over next week?"

"I don't know, sweethea . . . Brad." Snow falls outside the window, melting as it hits the ground.

"I'll make you an authentic homemade dinner." His smile is genuine. Not a hint of lechery.

"No," I say. "This one's on the house. You're a gentleman."

"I should pay you. This is a commodity exchange, after all."

"Not if we just talk. Conversation isn't worth anything. Shouldn't be."

"Well . . . I haven't . . . in a while. My wife left four nights ago. Took all her stuff."

I start the timer and reach for the toy on the bedside table.

"Just your hands," he says. "Slowly—like you're with someone you love."

I feel my temperature rising. My hips constrict and my legs arch and my breath leaves me, all of it, and for one beautiful moment I am only a body—I'm free.

"Was it good for you, too?" I ask.

That's when the door creaks open.

Auntie Rose stands in the doorway, deaf, looking at me, my body.

"We fought, you know that? We fought long and hard."

Shaming. I'm looking down from above.

"You're more than how you look."

The *m* lost between her teeth.

"Things are different now, Auntie Rose."

She can't hear me.

"Men will respect you if they see what you can do with your head."

All muffled, foggy, forgotten.

"Auntie!" Screaming, "What is it worth?"

The candles are perfect, and through their teasing flare I see Brad's face against the sparseness of his apartment. I see how beautiful it is, he is—how gentle, how warm. It's hard not to look at him as my ideal client. Maybe someone I could love.

"This is new for me," I say as he spoons salad onto my plate.

"What?"

"Sorry. Not used to being so . . . pampered."

Gentle? Caring? Why is that? Lack of work, manual labor, the kind that eluded my father? That pushed away my mother? That sustains my aunt?

He puts his knife down, wraps his hands around mine.

"I want to see what it's like. What you do, I mean. I want to see if it makes me . . ."

I lean in to meet his eyes. They're both reluctant. They're both scared, both . . . "Ashamed?"

"What?"

"Don't be ashamed."

I take his hand, lead him to his room.

I stand over him in his bed, a camera pointed at his face. "Are you nervous?"

He shakes his head, nods. I run my fingers down his chest. "Do you like it?"

He nods his head, shakes it.

I put his hands around the camera; he turns it around on me. When he does, I see a hollow void of aching pride; it swirls and lashes the lenses of my eyes. Rain blows against the window.

It *is* warm for January.

"What do you like, sweetheart?"

I pull off my shirt, slip off my heels.
Use your mind to make money, use your brain to make money.
"Do you like this?"
My jeans, my bra.
Took such a long time, you foolish little girl.
"Does this turn you on?"
Kneeling into the camera with nothing on me, in me.
You're not a commodity; you know that, right?

ERIN

Easter Sunday, 2013

When the tremors shook me awake, I walked to the park to score. The air stunk of pollen. I clawed my invisible rash and promised myself, again, to never wait till I got sick.

I dodged slush spit from the tires of passing cars as I wove down Hilton Road, and I knew I was right about everything. Needles worked up my spine and I coughed up bile outside of the old Dynamic Fabricating, watched the boarded windows sag with spring thaw.

After a few more blocks, I took a right and walked to Green Acres Park and saw him, sweatshirt hood up. The green grass quivered around him.

"Erin, right?"

I gave him a twenty.

He held out an orange bottle and I unscrewed the cap and ate three, right there. When my rash stopped screaming, I exhaled and sat down next to him.

"Beautiful day," he said. "Just beautiful."

"Can't wait for the rest of the snow to be gone." I played with the bottle in my jacket pocket and melted into the bench. On the other side of the park, Sunday school children from the church on Woodward Heights scavenged for Easter eggs.

"Why do you do this?"

"What?" he asked.

"Sorry." I closed my eyes, listened to the semis barrel down I-75. "When I'm high I do this thing where I ask myself questions and then say them out loud. I don't mean to."

"I'm just trying to get by."

"What?"

"To answer your question. I'm a pharm tech. They slashed our hours after the New Year. Corporate wants to keep the stock high. I might lose my house."

"Oh," I said. "Right." The kids chased each other through a jungle gym, jumped through metallic holes.

"So why do you?"

"Oh. God."

"Oh God what?"

I opened my eyes, rolled my head to face him. I was bathing in the swollen air, its sweet wretchedness.

I reached for his hand, intertwined our fingers. "This. Feel this."

"OK."

"Skin on skin. Do you think there's something other than this?"

"I guess I don't care."

"Most people don't." The kids joined hands and sang "Christ the Lord Is Risen Today."

"So you think we're, what, robots or something?"

"I mean we used to be, right? In Detroit and all. Robots that got paid well." The sun tried to break through the roof of gray clouds.

"I wouldn't know. I would have loved one of those jobs."

I laughed. "Love." I pulled my fingers away, slid them into my jacket. "Naw, there's nothing but us. This. People. Skin on skin."

"Sounds hopeless to me."

"You think you can love in a place like that?" The kids counted their eggs. Pinks, purples, yellows.

"Sure," he said. "That's the antidote."

"No way." I felt around my pocket for the bottle, held it up to him. "This is."

We sat there for a while, in that magic place where time evaporates.

DENNIS

Memorial

I wake up to the tornado siren, which reminds me what day it is—the first Saturday of the first week of the first month of summer. But without work, time doesn't mean much. The days weld together and the nights get longer and longer, even if I roll over and there's a blonde senior from Warren Fitzgerald curled up naked in my Red Wings throw, cheap mascara rubbed off on my pillow; even if it's dollar beers at the Stop Spot; even if my dad's driving down from Tawas with deer jerky; even if Steve calls and has night game Tigers tickets from his boss—which is happening today.

"Black Limousine" plays from my alarm clock, and I open the blinds to look at the street. That mangy cat the Cutters left behind when they moved to Indiana for that right-to-work bullshit yowls as I sip my coffee. I'm still young, and it doesn't seem that long ago that my neighborhood was more than just angry husbands and tired wives and kids who don't come home.

I open the fridge and sift through the condiments. At the very back I see a bottle of champagne from some new boutique winery up north. Janice gave it to me a few months back for us to open when I started working again. Attached to the bottle is a note: *Drink this to celebrate.* I think about tearing it off, not about her, then shove it back into place. Next to that is the ounce of weed one of the boys from the shop gave me when I told him I needed rent money and couldn't find work. "McDonald's is hiring," he said, and I punched him in the arm.

Shit, I think. There's nothing else to do.

"They're givin' Harry a stone." Mike tells me this in my backyard as Steve pours charcoal into the grill.

"A stone?" I say.

"Yup. Boys from the shop pitching together. Gonna put it out front."

"Which boys?"

"The ones who found some work. I'm chipping in a few bucks myself. Wish I had more to spare."

Mike's at Wayne State now, wants to teach labor history.

"I started an office pool for it," Steve says. "My buddy dropped off some stuff the other day." He looks at the ground, then out to the train yard. "Ropes and shit."

I should throw in, I think. I should sell that dope. I pull out my phone and text somebody and tell him to set up a deal down the street tonight.

"Bet he's drinkin' the saints under the table right now," Steve says.

"If it's anything like his wake down here," Mike says, and we laugh unhappily.

"God sounds great if you're poor—if you're dumb, don't He?" I ask.

"We ain't dumb. I'll say that much." Steve's full of shit—he's making a killing selling reverse mortgages to the old folks in our neighborhood who have burned through their Social Security too fast.

I stand up and light a smoke and put *Tattoo You* in the CD player.

"That siren's been going for two hours," Mike says.

Steve shrugs and opens another beer. "Maybe they're coming to finish us off."

Steve's always saying that now—newly affected pessimism.

"Nah, I don't think God likes us much," I continue. "If He did, He would've had the fuckin' Asians unionize."

We laugh and laugh. Then we stop and the siren cuts through the silence, rings our ears.

"Remember you on those fucking tie-downs?" Steve says. "We think it's hot today."

I loved that summer. I say that to myself. I'm afraid if I say it out loud the memory will escape and disappear, and I've had about enough of that.

It was scalding outside, and I sweated profusely, and I got a rash on my ass every day from sweating so much.

I was on tie-downs, which were a part of fenders for all-purpose vehicles. I took these Texas-shaped plates and put them on a rotating metal stand in stacks of fifty. I heated them up with an oxygen and propane torch till they were molten in the center, then grabbed them one by one with thick leather welding gloves and put them in the press brake, flipping the sides up, over and over. I did 700 a day, every day, all summer. Hard work in the shop—we earned our goddamn money. It was Mike's uncle's place, and I worked on the shop floor with Harry and Steve. Harry and I gave Mike shit all the time because I was on tie-downs and Harry was deburring, taking the sharp edges off of steel from the fabricator with a belt sander. Steve was stuck at the drill press putting holes in axles while Mike got to go outside, out back, organizing dies with the hi-low. We tried to piss him off—called him "Prince" a lot because he was probably going to get a cut if his uncle sold it. If the place went under.

We woke up at 5 a.m. and burned our tongues chugging coffee and sucking down cigarettes as we drove in the thick of blue-collar rush hour, people going to the eastside factories belching smoke and hissing from air hoses.

On some of my breaks I walked out to Hilton to get some fresh air—fresh as it could be in Ferndale in the summer with those car fumes pasted in the air by the humidity. I looked both ways down the two-lane highway, either side of me stretching out flat—the endless plains of shops and plants and factories, pickup trucks and semis hurtling toward each other, then away, leaving clouds of exhaust floating up to the sun, the searing furnace that purged us clean every day.

When the bell rang at three on Fridays, we'd go straight to the liquor store across the street with Harry's fake ID and buy beer with our paychecks. We had a few in the back, singing whatever catchy song was on the radio with the windows down, our ears popping with hard bursts of warm air. If we pulled up to a red light and there was a rusty Sebring filled with the girls from high school who went off to college, the smart girls that appreciated fast love at home, quick hot summer romance, fierce and sticky with desire, we would toss them some beer and make fun of their makeup and wind up in their living rooms with our shirts off as they rubbed the oil and grime from our necks.

That's how I met Janice, and thinking of it now, even though it's scrambled by the beer and the siren, I almost feel sorry for letting her down.

"Eat up." Steve doles out the first round of hot dogs.

"Hope the boys are OK," Mike says.

"Wouldn't worry about them," I say. "Worry about your poor uncle."

"Fuck off," he says, jokingly.

"Where's he live now—Bloomfield Hills?"

"With all the other carpetbaggers." Steve snickers to himself and checks the time on his new watch.

"He's not a carpetbagger," Mike says apologetically. "Victim of the global market. I went to a seminar on campus about it last week. The long, slow decline of American manufacturing."

"That's not true," I say, flipping open another top. "Came out of nowhere."

But *that's* not true. We knew it was coming. Sixty hours down to fifty, to forty, to thirty-two so we could keep our benefits, pink slips, unemployment checks cashed at the liquor store.

Harry saw it before it happened.

"They say this is gonna hurt for a while," he said, and we called him an asshole. He said we should enlist with him; said that our work drying up meant the war in Iraq was finished, that all the mountains in Afghanistan meant you had a lower chance of getting shot.

"Gonna get paid to do nothing, and we can come back when all this is better."

We told him he was taking the easy way out.

"Rather that than become a criminal," he said.

"Had the weirdest client this week," Steve says.

"Don't get me started on weird," Mike says. "This one chick in a class I'm TAing kept opening her legs when I was giving a lecture on the UAW."

"Sounds like good work, fellas." I am getting drunk.

. . .

Dynamic Fabricating, that was work, man. That was *work*. If we got a hot job that gave us a seventy-hour week we would peel out of the lot on Saturday at two, exhausted and dreaming of how we were gonna blow all that overtime. How good that new rifle would chew up deer shoulders up north in the fall—how good the inside of the classy girls at the bar would feel when I was loaded on Maker's Mark, staying hard all night without the woody bullshit we choked down before we got the job.

God, did that feel good.

Steve and Mike talking about their jobs bores me, so I climb a ladder to the roof and stand on my toes, and when I look south I can see the shop and my heart gets light and I think to myself, *Goddamn, how could anyone think this is ugly. How could anyone hate this?* I can see us, how it was, how I wish it still was, how bad I want Harry back. I'll never tell Steve or Mike that this lonely view is the reason why I moved to this street, this house. They wouldn't understand.

"Any leads, Den?" Steve asks when I come back down.

I shake my head.

Mike laughs. "Still waiting to punch in, huh?"

"The fuck's so funny about that?" For a second I get angry, really angry, like I want to scrap with Mike like in the old days.

Then I think of this thing I wrote down a few nights ago after putting "Heaven" on loop:

"Don't care about, don't need it. Is some broad gonna drive into town and buy the factory? Is some chick gonna get me my job back? That's a girl I would go after, suffer for. That's a girl I would love. C'mon. Be real. She ain't comin'. And even if she did, wouldn't be nothing like the first time."

"The fuck's that about?" Steve asks.

"Huh?"

"What you just said."

I didn't realize I was talking. "Just a . . . memorial, I guess. If I died, I dunno . . ." I take another sip of beer.

"You're gettin' sentimental on us." Mike adjusts his khakis. "Is it about Janice?"

"Sure."

Steve checks his smartphone for updates on the broken siren.

"Fancy," I say. He's getting annoyed, like he did at the shop when he was too hot or too tired. The siren blares between my ears as that mangy cat limps across the lawn. It's like it lives there now, and I start walking for it, saying, *here kitty kitty*. Mike says, "Dennis, man, let it go." I tell him you can't look at life like that, that the cat didn't do anything.

"Some things you gotta let die."

Steve says he has to make a business call and goes inside. Mike stays quiet, and I hate that, the silence, so I start talking.

"I used to think the routine was horrifying. Something that sucked away your essence, yeah, because that whole shit about a soul or a spirit or hope, that's all bullshit, that doesn't exist. You should feel lucky to breathe."

"If you say so."

"Now I want one. I want to get up early and hit my alarm and say *fuck this*, drown my hangover in Maxwell House and eat my Twinkie in the car listening to the morning show on 97.1. I want to suck down a Camel and have the smoke leak out my nose before I punch in and nod mornin' to the lazy assholes twice my age. I want to pull my earplugs out at breakfast and close my eyes and listen to the semis on I-75 and imagine I'm by the water as I inhale the exhaust . . ."

"That another epitaph?"

"Thanks for the support."

"What the fuck are you so romantic for, anyway? That place sucked. That job sucked. It was hot and dirty, and we were fucking tired all the time. We spent all our money on our cars and booze and girls. It was a race into the fucking sun, Den. Now some other poor bastards will do it until they cost too much, and then some other poor bastards will, and one day it'll wind up back at the shop, when we're all old."

"They tell you all that in class, smart guy?"

Steve walks out to the porch and asks if we're leaving.

"Nah." I shake my head and look at the ground.

"We should hurry. Just got a text from a client—we could get in his suite if we get down there soon."

"Oh fuck you, Steve," I say. "Getting your raises off the backs of old ladies."

He doesn't even get pissed, just shakes his head and says, "Welcome to the New Economy."

"*Fuck you*," I say, though I don't mean it, not in relation to Steve, anyway. The beer's gone to my head and that goddamn siren won't stop wailing. I fumble for my cigarettes and feel the bag of pot.

That's right, I remember. That's right.

"Let's go, Mike. I wanna make it down there before we're too drunk."

I shield my eyes from the sun and look down at Steve's shoes and see how fucking shiny they are, how embarrassed he would be if he saw himself now two years ago.

My phone buzzes and I flip it open. The text reads: *Kady's at 10. 2 college kids.* I'm not drunk enough to forget the deal—not drunk enough to forget the stone.

I tell my old friends I'll meet them there. Errands to run, bullshit.

When they leave, I take the rest of the beer up to the roof and watch the sun set in the west, fading light reflected on windshields. When it's dark and the beer's gone, I hop down and lock the door. I shoo the cat away, the siren still crying, and as I make my way to the bar it's like I can see the nights stretching down Nine Mile, that goddamn flat road—see them stretching on and on and knowing that in those long nights are long dreams about the things I've loved and the things that scare me. How all those dreams will be the same, just getting longer with the nights until the loves and fears grow patchy and fade—until they're forgotten and all that's left are guttural twinges when diesel fumes waft through my open window and dissolve in the curtains.

· · ·

I haven't been to Kady's in ages—the hipsters found out about it, and since those spoiled brats raise prices wherever they go, I can't afford to get drunk there anymore. But as I walk up Nine Mile and wade through the parking lot and open the back door, the same old smell hits me—urine and cigarettes and cheap beer—and for the first time in a while, I feel like myself. I take a seat at the end of the bar and play with the bag in my pocket. All this, I think to myself, just 'cause I don't want to be like Mike, like Steve, like . . .

Some guy walks in with a beat-up pair of Red Wings and dirty fingernails and I feel a familiar pang of jealousy.

As I wait for my customers, I sip beer and watch the bartender, some girl back home from school I think I recognize. I try to trace her past or what I imagine it to be from when I last saw her to now, flipping off bottle caps and pouring well shots. Mick Jagger sings, "*Ain't no use in crying. Stay away from me*," from the jukebox, and I remember how I always hated listening to the end of that album, how fucking sad it was.

But Harry loved the B side of *Tattoo You*, said it was an extended lullaby, and since he's been gone, I've put it on when I can't sleep and it's like he's with me again, with us.

"What do you want tonight, sweetheart?" I look up at the bartender, pretty and young.

"Some work," I say.

She thinks it's funny, flicks the curls out of her eyes. "What kinda work?" she asks, and when I lean in to lay it on, the back door opens and three kids walk in. Someone's brought backup, I think to myself. They aren't as old as they said they were. They look like children, and they have just walked into something they don't understand.

I lick my lips.

I take a shot and walk up to the biggest one—Oxford shirt and chino shorts, close-cropped hair.

"Can I help you?" I ask. It's not a question, really.

"Looking for Dennis," the big one says.

I look over and see his friend, false confidence in the absence of height, and when my eyes wander down past his eyes, I notice his dark blue work shirt with a greased nametag whose name I can't make out.

"Where'd you buy that shirt, tough guy?"

"Value World."

"Uh-huh." He's getting nervous and I'm getting angry. "You ever work with your hands?"

The third skinny friend starts laughing.

"What do you mean?"

I take his hands and turn them over, noticing the perfect fingernails, the covered veins, the absence of scars.

"Nah."

"My grandpa used to own a factory around here."

"I bet he did."

They're quiet now, all three of them, their petty confidence absorbed by the stench, the dull roar of the workers getting drunk on a Friday night.

"Let's go."

Walking back to the parking lot, I look at their necks and their clean-ness turns my stomach. I'm flooded with rage, with shame. I'm a crimi-nal. I grab an ashtray off the bar and empty it on the floor.

That's when I notice the quiet; the siren has stopped.

"You lucky bastard," I say.

"What?"

I punch the big guy in the mouth with the ashtray; he falls on his knees, spits out some blood.

The skinny guy puts his hands up like he's being arrested, his bottom lip starts shaking *no, no*. I smile and raise my arm. He bolts for the car.

It's just me and the one with the money.

"Some friends," I say.

"Why?" The fear hollows his eyes. "I just . . ."

"You just *what*?" I take two steps toward him till he's against the wall. No running.

"Can't you just . . . Can't I just . . ."

"Just what?"

"If you hurt me, I'll tell the cops. My dad's a . . ."

"You're in the middle of a drug deal," I say, and that just about cripples him. "There is no law right now. It's just me and you."

He tries to stand tough, defiant. I bet he's on the football team at his private school, big shot slumming it for a rush, and would take my shit back home telling his friends how tough he is now.

But his hands are shaking.

"Give me your wallet, tough guy."

He hands it over.

"Please, just . . ."

I put a right hook in his kidney and that drops him quick. His buddy's getting to his feet now, shirt stained in blood, nose dripping snot.

"Sit the fuck down." And he does.

I take all the money out of the wallet—$200 in cash—and sit down between them and light a cigarette.

"I'm sorry, guys. I'm not usually like this." I exhale.

The kids are silent. The last fight I ever had was with Steve the night Harry left. We soaked our knuckles in beer the next day on the way back from the airport.

"My best friend died last month, in Afghanistan. Neither of you would know what that feels like. I'm sure neither one of you even knows someone over there."

They try to catch their breaths.

"Well *do* you?"

They shake their heads, no.

"Well, it ain't a good feeling. But to be honest with you guys, it's not really the KIA thing . . . kinda, but not really."

I exhale.

"And it's kinda that they're building a memorial to him, right down that road over there . . ." I point down the alley to Nine Mile, curl my fingers to Hilton, "but not really."

"No, the thing that makes me so upset, is that that guy, my friend . . ." I tense up and then relax. I feel exhausted. "I'm jealous." It feels good to say it. "I'm jealous."

The cigarette's at the filter and I flick it away. I pick the two rich kids up by their collars and toss them into the parking lot.

"Nothin' personal, fellas." I throw them back their money. "This ain't your fault. Well, maybe a little."

I walk back into the bar to take one last shot. I don't see them peel out.

The walk home is beautiful, my favorite time of year in Ferndale. Stars out, cool breeze kissing you through humid air. Take a deep breath crossing Woodward and you might even get a taste of the damp filth of the Detroit River all the way down there—if the wind's blowing up from the water.

But that's miles and miles away, and there's only one place I'm going: straight down the middle of Nine Mile, splitting the lanes, tightrope walking the yellow lines all the way to Hilton, to the old façade of Dynamic Fabricating.

Then I remember Janice's bottle, how cold and useless it is in the fridge by itself. I stop in and grab it, singing "Hang Fire" to myself until I feel something against my leg.

"Hey stranger," I say.

It purrs as it slaloms between my feet.

"Just 'cause you got left behind . . . that don't mean a damn thing."

I pick it up and hold it in my arms, smooth out its knotted fur.

"Nah, ain't so bad. You're still alive."

I make my way down Hilton and cut through the train yard.

"We're gonna have a drink with an old friend."

It's roped off already, four pegs and blue velvet.

I step over and stand in the middle, right on the spot that stone's going to be, and the cat leaps down as I uncork the champagne and pour it out, all of it, right on the fresh green summer grass, the indelible civic memory of Harold Plummer.

There you go, Golden Boy. You took the easy way out.

PETE

Devil's Night

In Social Studies, the principal comes over the PA and gives the same speech he does every October 30, telling us about the 10 p.m. curfew, the stepped-up patrol and neighborhood watch, to not disgrace our city or our school or ourselves. When he's done, our teacher Mr. Thomas gives us his two cents. He tells us about how Devil's Night started after the '67 riots, how it's Detroit's unique holiday, how it used to be the worst on the east side, where, one night in the eighties, a thousand structures went up in flames.

"Fuckin' dumbass probably lives on the east side of Ferndale," my friend Tommy says under his breath, though he does, too. So do I. "The fuck does he know about it?"

"What's the point?" I say, pulling the zipper of my jacket. "The only reason the numbers have gone down is 'cause there's nothing left to burn."

Victor laughs behind us, sorting candy he stole from homeroom earlier. "There's a little bit left. You just gotta scope it out, that's all."

Chris laughs at Victor, rubs the sleep from his eyes. "We should burn down *your* house," he says.

"My house is nice, man," Victor says, adjusting the brim of his fitted Tigers hat. "Bigger than Mr. Thomas's, that's for sure."

The class laughs. Mr. Thomas brushes it off, returns to his lecture.

"This dovetails nicely with our discussion. Drugs fill the economic hole left by industrial work. This inevitably leads to substance abuse, particularly alcoholism, which then leads to jail sentences that, as the system is now constructed, prevent the incarcerated from ever again attaining gainful employment."

Victor throws a miniature candy bar at him when he turns to write something on the board. He turns back and yells at us, louder, but by then we're all laughing. He shakes his head and passes out our homework and sits down at his desk.

Chris crumples his up, pops one of Victor's stolen Milky Ways in his mouth. "Come on, man. He's doing his best."

"Why the fuck do they have a twenty-three-year-old teaching seniors?" Victor asks.

Tommy taps his drumsticks on his thigh. "I don't think he had a choice. Would you want to teach us?"

I feel bad for him, too, but don't say anything. As the class talks Halloween plans for tomorrow, who's doing what where, I look down at the prompt: *What are the differences in opportunity between your parents at your age and you?*

Tommy and I stop by Victor's locker after class to buy a quarter ounce of weed before Victor's lunch rush. Chris puts his backpack in his locker and grabs his Little Caesars hat and apron.

"You're a clown," Victor says to Chris.

"At least I have a real job," Chris says, throwing his essay on the floor of his locker.

"Right," Victor says. "A 'real' job that pays you eight bucks an hour."

But that's about as much as my mom makes. Tommy's mom and my mom work the late shift at the same dollar store in the mini-mall where Sears and Farmer Jack used to be. They've had to work since that fabricating shop on Hilton closed and our dads packed up and split.

Tommy sees his girlfriend and they walk away, both muttering, looking at the ground. I stand off to the side as some Pleasant Ridge kids walk up to Victor.

"You're a lifesaver, man," they tell him. "College campus visits all weekend. Spending forty-eight hours with my parents? Fuck, will that stress me out."

"I bet it will," Victor says, winking at Chris and me.

Tommy walks back to the lockers, stands next to me, checks his phone. "Your dad call you yet?"

I shake my head. Since he left, he calls me every Devil's Night once he's had enough to drink. He thinks it's funny, for whatever reason—I can never understand him that well. Never could.

"At least he still calls you," Chris says behind us. "Haven't heard from mine since last Christmas."

"He still sends you money every month, right?" Tommy asks Chris.

Chris laughs. "Why do you think I'm working?"

"Are they hiring?" I ask Chris. Money's been tight at home—my mom's been on my ass about getting an after-school job if I'm not playing sports.

Victor walks back to his locker, then coughs, smiles at me. "You short, Pete?"

"Maybe."

"You guys got my number, right?" he asks Tommy and me.

We nod.

"I might have a job for you. You wanna make a few bucks, have some fun tonight, gimme a call."

After school, Tommy and I sit in my living room playing video games. Every few minutes, I put down my controller and scribble notes in response to Mr. Thomas's prompt:

> *I can't be my father; even if I really knew him, even if I wanted to be . . . I don't drink, neither do my friends, my dad . . . our dads . . . started drinking after they lost their jobs . . .*

Tommy plugs his phone into my speakers and plays tracks from his SoundCloud—a new project he calls *Post-Industrial:* electronica spliced with live drums punctuated with silences recorded in the concrete husks that shadow our neighborhood.

He lights a joint filled with Victor's weed. "Pretty good, right?"

"Put that out, man," I tell him. "You can't smoke in the house."

"Your mom smokes."

"I don't care. Put it out."

"Relax, Pete. Jesus." He throws it out the window. "Really though—what do you think of the new stuff?"

I pause the game and listen to the staccato hi-hats ripple through the somber flap of crow wings. "Not bad." I nod my head to the beat and look out the window at the little kids coming home from the elementary school across the street, pulling keys out from under rocks and letting themselves in the side doors of their small houses covered with fake cobwebs and cardboard tombstones. I wonder where my dad is, what kind of buddy-buddy nonsense he's gonna mumble through the phone tonight. I turn the game back on.

"You going over to Stephanie's?" I ask him.

"Not tonight." He exhales.

"Have you guys told your parents?"

"Haven't decided what to do yet."

"Huh."

"I wish I studied more. Can't raise a kid with a diploma job."

"It's too late for us, anyway."

"What, grade-wise?"

"Well, our dads raised us on diploma jobs."

"Fuck them," Tommy says, eyes on the floor.

Through their living room windows, I watch the kids trying on their costumes for tomorrow night—cheap video game character outfits from the dollar store my mom works at.

Tommy looks up at me. "What do you think about tonight?"

"What about tonight?"

"That 'job' Victor was talking about. You think we should check it out?"

"I don't know."

"What—you scared or something?"

"Fuck you."

"What else are we gonna do? Walk up and see our moms? Buy some chalky Halloween candy? Get a fuckin' costume?"

"Write this essay, man."

Tommy laughs. "You're joking, right?"

"What did you just say to me?"

"What did *you*?"

I don't say anything.

"We could both use the money, Pete."

We both stare at the TV for a while, the bass pulsing through the floorboards, then Tommy calls Victor.

He drives over at midnight.

"Nice house," he says.

"Thanks," I say. I don't tell him it's a rental.

"Parents home?"

"My mom doesn't get home till late."

"What about your dad?"

We all laugh—even though we don't know *where* they are, we know where they are.

Victor shrugs. He looks over at a picture of my mom and me from when we went down to Cedar Point last summer.

"That your mom?"

I nod.

He laughs. "She's young."

"She's hot," Tommy says, and I punch him in the shoulder.

"Your mom's the same age, dickhead," I tell him. That's true—they were pregnant with Tommy and me at the same time after high school.

"So," Victor says, pulling the strings of his Carhartt, "you guys down for an adventure tonight?"

"If it pays," Tommy says.

"It'll be worth your time. I promise." Victor turns to me. "Where's your liquor cabinet?"

I lead Victor to the kitchen and open the alcove above the sink. He reaches all the way back and grabs two leftover bottles of Everclear from my mom's Labor Day party. I've never touched any of it—my dad got out of control with it before he left, and I don't want to risk developing the same habit. Victor hands me a white T-shirt that's lying on a stool.

"Rip it in half," he says. I do.

He takes the two pieces and gives one to each of us.

"When I tell you when, soak the shirt with the liquor then stuff it back in. When you're ready to throw it, light the part that's sticking out."

"What do we need these for?" I ask.

Victor smiles. "Think of it as . . . as a useful tool for tonight."

We tuck the bottles under our jackets.

"We're gonna have a blast," he says.

On the way out, I pull Tommy back and let Victor walk ahead.

"Are you sure about this?" I say.

He pushes me away. "Come on. It'll be fun."

We drive down my street and then up Nine Mile and stop at a red light.

"Last chance to get out," Victor says, lighting a joint and passing it around.

We don't say anything. I feel around for the ripped T-shirt, pull out my essay instead.

My parents had me after they graduated from Ferndale–my dad had a job lined up at Dynamic Fabricating, a mortgage . . . When you mentioned alcohol and jail earlier, the first thing I thought of was my dad, of all his DUIs, the assault charges from his bar fights. He can't drive anymore, so can't work anymore, but before his shop closed . . . before that place closed . . . Anyways, I feel like a nuisance to my mom, that I just remind her of him, about what she lost . . . he lost . . .

I try to concentrate, but the weed's gone to my head, the memories bleeding into each other. Victor stares at me through the rearview mirror. "Some dude—one of my clients—paid me a thousand bucks to burn down that old shop on Nine Mile and Hilton tonight. Says if there's enough fire damage he can buy the property from the bank for nothing."

"What's he gonna do with it?" Tommy asks.

"Fuck if I know. Probably luxury condos or some bullshit like that. None of my business."

I've started to notice them around the east side of the city. It's been five years since the recession hit and Dynamic closed up, and I've seen plenty of rusted factories converted into spacious lofts. I've been wondering who has a half million dollars to drop on those things or why they would want to live there in the first place.

I take a long hit, and as I exhale, I realize where we're going.

"Dynamic Fabricating?" I ask.

I see Victor nod in the rearview mirror.

"Revenge," Tommy says, taking the joint from my fingers.

We wind through the side streets and stop by Little Caesars to pick up Chris. He gets in the car next to me and takes off his vest. He has dark circles under his eyes and reeks of pizza dough.

"You ready?" Victor asks, smiling.

Chris shakes his head and says, "Sure," and we shoot through the parking lot, down Hilton, toward the shop.

We light another joint as we inch closer and closer, the streetlights glowing on the windshield. Tommy plugs his phone into the tape deck converter and mouths the bass lines, the noise filling my head, my mouth drying up. Chris's leg starts twitching. He looks over at me. "I asked my boss if there were any openings. Told me you can stop in any time and fill out an application."

Victor passes Chris the joint. "He doesn't need that bullshit job."

"Shut up," Chris says. "I don't know if this is a good idea. Won't the cops be patrolling?"

"They axed the night shift last year to save money. I told you that already."

Chris sucks in his chest and looks at Victor. "You're not gonna do it."

"Shut up, man. I already took the money. Can't back out now."

"Then don't do it."

"I told you to shut up, Chris."

"Let me out of the car, Victor."

Victor doesn't answer. He looks ahead at the hollowed shell of Dynamic in the distance and turns up the music.

"Let me out!" Chris yells.

It takes me a while to turn my head, but when I do, I look over to the passenger seat at Tommy. His eyes are wide open, eyebrows twitching.

"I'm getting out of the car," Chris says.

"No, you're not," Victor snaps back.

"Yes, I am."

Victor locks the doors and turns the music up again, lights another joint. The bass shakes the teeth in the back of my jaw.

Victor stops the car at a red light. Chris unlocks the door and gets out.

"Get the fuck back in the car, man! Easiest money you'll ever make!"

Chris slams the door and takes off down a street.

Victor leans over and yells out the window. "All right then, bitch! All right! Walk the fuck home, coward!"

The light turns green and we speed forward, and I watch Chris disappear in the rearview mirror.

We snake through the alleys and park in the back of the loading dock. Abandoned cars stuffed with tin cans and ragged sleeping bags litter the parking lot, windows gone. It's dark outside except for the quartered moon. Victor turns the headlights off. He gets out quietly, then pops the trunk and pulls out two five-gallon gas cans. Tommy and I get out with our bottles.

I look around the lot, then past rusty fences to the jack-o'-lanterns shimmering on the porches of the surrounding bungalows. We're all alone. I tuck the bottle under my jacket and walk up to the bay doors.

They used to be painted some neutral color; at least, that's what I think as I look at them. All the windows are broken. It already looks burnt.

Victor pulls a hammer from his jacket. He breaks off the padlock and lifts the door.

There are a few pieces of old ripped-up furniture on the main floor. Moonlight breaks through the jagged glass of the windows and spills onto the dusty concrete, flecks of epoxy spitting light at us. I stare through the weed's hazy filter at beer cans, liquor bottles, cigarette butts, discarded ends of joints, blunts. The walls are torn open where the copper wire's been pulled out.

Victor starts pouring gas on the floor, on piles of squatters' garbage, broken pallets used for firewood. Tommy and I watch him as he works. I remember, briefly, coming here with my dad years ago, a company party or Bring Your Child to Work Day, standing on the spot where my dad showed me how he ground off bubbled material from bad welds that Victor now pours gas on.

When Victor's done, we walk together up the creaking staircase to the manager's offices.

"Chris's dad used to work up here," Victor says. "I think that's where he gets his attitude about work from. Management will do that to you."

Victor splashes gas on everything and then leaves the room with Tommy. I stay and sit down on the floor and try to breathe; my heart is beating out of my chest and my mouth is arid from Victor's joints. I reach into my jacket to feel the pumping blood and find my essay in the breast pocket. In the corner of the office, I see an old dresser, oak or some other fine wood with clean edges, brass knobs, its dusty mirror intact. It's the same my mom has in her bedroom. I uncap a pen.

My grandma took this beautiful dresser with her when she left the city after the '67 riots and gave it to my mom as a wedding present; she still does her hair in front of it before she goes to work in the afternoon or the bar on her day off on Saturday night . . .

I brush the dust from the mirror, stare at my refection.

I wonder how she looked . . . at herself . . . to herself . . . if opportunity, or the lack of it, leaves marks on your face . . . scars that set your dreams in time . . .

I look at the walls of the room, covered with graffiti. I try to decipher the scripted letters, the handiwork of one of the crews from school until I hear Victor yelling downstairs, telling me he's done and we need to get out. I pull out my bottle of Everclear and leave the room. And as the gas leaks into my socks, I think that the three of us *should* be here—eighteen, sick of school, bored and frustrated and ready to work like our fathers eighteen years ago; we *should* be here, high, in one way or another, moving from station to station, fashioning raw metals into something they're not.

"Hey." It's Tommy's hand on my shoulder. "You OK?"

But we *are* here working, we are here.

"I'm fine." I try to listen for the noises of my dad, but I only hear Victor mouthing the bass lines of Tommy's new songs, the cadence perfectly matching my conclusion to Mr. Thomas's essay:

I can never be my father, even if I wanted to.

We walk outside to the curb then turn to face the building. We reek of fuel. I look around and check for other people, listen for sirens before I remember what Victor said about the night shift and realize our principal lied to us about the extra cops. It's silent.

Victor looks at me. "Let's light it up."

I nod my head.

Victor looks at Tommy, who's shaking.

"Come on, man. Do it," Victor says.

Tommy tries to twist the cap off his bottle, but his hands are shaking too much.

I stand there with my own bottle, struggling with its weight. I twist the top off, reaching into my pocket for the half rag Victor gave me. I pause, then put the rag back and stuff in my essay instead.

"Do it!"

Tommy stands next to me and tugs at my bottle. I think I hear him say something, but all I can think about is my dad.

I grab the lighter from Victor, light the paper, and throw the bottle.

The floor catches, burning a bright blue. It reaches the piles of trash, but they're too wet to catch. The pallet splinters smolder, but they've already exhausted their use.

Within a few minutes, the gas has burned out, evaporated. Just the smell remains—hot garbage, rotten wood.

I look over at Tommy. He's still shaking.

Victor stands silently. I look at his face, covered in gas and sweat, and I can't tell if he's crying. "You were right," he says.

"What are you talking about?" I ask.

"In class earlier. There's nothing left to burn."

We linger in the bay opening for a while, not speaking, listening to the cars on the freeway. Then we pull the doors down, get back in the car, and drive away.

The car ride home is silent. Victor keeps the stereo off, hands us our share of the money. "Don't tell anybody about this, understand?"

We nod.

When we get to my house, Tommy and I get out and watch Victor's car gun through stop signs as it disappears down the street.

We don't say anything to each other. I give him the bag of weed and he walks home.

I walk inside and find a note from my mom saying she's out at the bar. I turn off the lights, sit down on the couch, and wait for the phone to ring.

ALEX

The Slow Death

"Read it again," I ask her. "I want to hear it in person." We keep our distance on the walk from the Amtrak station on Woodward to my apartment in the cold silence of the night. I take her in—the dyed black hair, the green eyes, the scent I can't place. She reaches into the breast pocket of her winter coat, pulls out folded paper.

> I can't describe dispossession
> the way some can paint it.
> What words would do justice
> to two faces, wan and creased
> with anxiety, exhaustion
> that I've seen so often,
> that I've worn myself?
> Like the man on the left,
> resting on a tattered sportscoat,
> too worried for sleep,
> cloaked in scattered
> rags, dispatches from
> high society used for
> tonic or warmth or both.
> It doesn't matter when
> you're that tired,
> bruised from the world.
> Any comfort will do.
>
> Swimmers dive in the background,
> naked, fleshy.

The contrast of their joy
(or indifference)
is striking.
Around them empty boats steam by,
like tourists around this painting,
pausing to pity these men
then look at something else.
I've seen hundreds
with faces like these two,
avoided or ignored by
averted eyes.
Poverty is leprosy
to those in possession,
the thought of its loss
too abstract, too insane.

I hear those passing people
talk rapturously about a life
without possessions.
As always, it is
material possessions in question,
that they aren't needed
to live a material life
fully and without concern.
And my anger's tempered only
by the knowledge
that these people have never been
dispossessed,
have never owned something
purchased through labor
that is not material,
that the possession of labor itself
is the bulwark against absurdity.

The man on the right,
old socks exposing
thin aging legs—he
looks at nothing.
He wears a suit
he no longer needs,
now just the uniform
of the dispossessed.

"I love it," I say. "It's gorgeous."

"It's called *On the East River*. It was hanging in a museum," she says. "The painting, I mean. In Minneapolis."

My stomach tightens. I stare at the ground. "I guess I don't need to see it now."

She reaches for my hand. I hold it.

She points out the mural in progress on the corner of Cass and Willis. "What is that?"

"Graffiti. Someone's trying to make a carbon copy of the city in the '60s."

She looks down Cass to the buildings downtown, past the gutted houses, the weeds and broken glass.

I want to say, *I missed you. I missed you so much I forgot you.*

In bed, she tells me she's an angel and I say, "Yeah, right."

"Really." She pulls my fingers across the bones of her shoulder blades. "Don't you feel them?"

"Feel what?"

"My wings, stupid." The smell of exhaust sifts through the window on the back of cold air.

"Delia?" It's the first time I've said her name in five years.

"Yes, Alex?" The first time she's said mine.

"Do you think this is a good idea?" I run my fingers across her back, feeling for her wings. We're in the dark with the blinds drawn and can't see each other—something she says we used to do together, a long time ago.

"Do you?" We take off each other's clothes and discard them, hearing them land softly on the floor.

"Let's not talk about it." We pull each other close. "Let's not talk at all."

"I had the strangest dream last night." Darren sits next to Lisa and looks out the window of American House nursing home, over the scattered factories and bungalows.

I open my notepad. "They've been vivid recently."

"Right, that's right. I can't remember all of it . . ."

Though he's repeated this for weeks now, I never get tired of hearing it. "Just what you can," I say. "What you can write about."

"OK. I'm on my bike—I'm sixteen in 1965. I'm riding through the factories in the evening. It must be Friday because people are peeling out of the lots and bells ring intermittently. I ride and I ride and the sounds grow and swell until it's like an orchestra before the sun sinks below the smokestacks and casts their shadows over Ferndale, Hazel Park, the east side, and all the way down to Detroit. My legs are sore from pedaling as I watch the sun set, and I realize it's the first day of summer."

It's quiet for a while.

"And then?" Lisa asks.

"And then I wake up."

"That's beautiful," I tell him, and realize that beauty, or the warm, lustrous sense of it Darren has created in my mind, was lying with me last night, familiar in a lost way. "You know I used to live near the place you're describing, right?"

"Did you?" He shakes his head and smiles. "You must have told me that a million times. Sorry I keep forgetting." He rubs his hands when he scans his memories, and I'm always impressed by their strength, their thickness earned from thirty years at a press brake. I can see in the way he moves his arms that he hasn't forgotten the motions, the repetitions that have become a reflex he can't remember he learned.

Lisa pats him on the hands and brushes gray curls from her eyes.

"Never say *sorry* for that." She points to a sentence I wrote in her notepad when we started the writing group—a ten-week session I facilitate, helping them leave a written legacy for their children, their grandchildren.

"That's right, Lisa. Let's begin. Darren, were you able to interpret the dream? Your writing is getting more surreal, more expressive."

He smiles. "I have something in here from last week, I think."

As he scans his pages, Lisa looks out the window at the cold, spotty clouds coughing up sunshine. She used to be an amateur meteorologist back in her receptionist days at Dynamic Fabricating down the road, tracking the barometric pressure on her meal breaks, noting the slant of the sun.

Then one year her boss took a look at her sketches and saw the same day repeated over and over and over, and now she's here at American House in Hazel Park, where she can look at Dynamic, now empty, and try to remember the wind patterns.

"Sorry, gang!" Sam opens the door and limps to his seat. "I forgot what time we met today."

Sam's got a busted knee, torn meniscus from a hi-low accident at work years ago. He forgets about it when he wakes up in the morning until the pain returns. He always smiles and apologizes as he limps in late after his caretaker asks him to check his calendar.

"You're just in time," I say.

There's been more work on the mural—details in the windows of the buildings downtown. The Detroit River is reflected off the glass of the Penobscot Building, the Guardian Building. I get up close and run my fingers over them, amazed at the level of detail possible with spray cans.

"Good day?"

I barely hear her voice. I'm still hearing Darren's—not his really, the voice his writing creates. It floats like an aria in the empty space of my apartment.

"Yeah." I watch her pull her socks off. "I think they're trying too hard to remember at times, but their writing is getting more concrete."

"The salon I filled out an application for today, down the street? I told them about your patients." Her socks off now—she curls her toes. "They said they couldn't do what you do." She holds her legs in the air. "Said it would crush them."

"The only sad thing, to me, I guess, is how healthy they are. Like their bodies aren't decaying, their faces are barely creased." She sits behind me, pulls off my shirt. "But it makes what we're doing that much more important. They're leaving themselves on a page while their memories fade . . . they'll never really die."

She runs her fingers across my lower stomach, smooths out the stretch marks, pinches loose skin.

"What happened here?"

"I get hungry when I'm sad." I take her hands and fold them in mine. "And I got sad when you left."

She pulls off her shirt and brings my hand to her ribs.

"Feel for it."

I run my fingers across the bones, horizontally, stopping to feel the cartilage between.

"What's that?" I press a bruise and she flinches. "Did you break a rib?"

"Failed attempt at gymnastics. I get bored when I'm alone."

My fingers roll along her back. "Why did you come back?"

"For you." She smiles. I don't. "I missed . . ." She looks out the window, to the cold evening light refracted by the Renaissance Center. "I don't know. This place is all I can write about. My subject is here."

She stretches and I see a scar between her bra straps. "Is that . . . ?"

She unhooks it and I run my hand across it.

"Fourth of July. Don't you remember?"

I pull back my fingers and swallow.

"Lake Huron, bottle rockets, too much wine." When it doesn't register, she shakes her head. "We wrote about it." She walks to her suitcase, pulls out a discolored folder, walks it back to me. "Read it," she says.

Calloused, you are, like me;
rough with singed edges we
can never hide.
We buried our grieves years ago
in Gallic wine with
gilded labels whose
vintage made us sick.
It suited us, you said.
I padded my embraces with down
to shield you from my coarseness.
You hewed away the cushions
and we grated, skin on skin,
too jagged to mourn with others.

She leans in and kisses me. She picks up the folder, fans the pages. "Do you still write?"

Not since you left. "Just some poetry here and there. When I have time."

"Should I still call you that?" She turns me around, wraps her legs where her arms used to be. "A poet?"

I watch the covers mold to her shape. "You can call me whatever you want."

We kiss again, harder this time, and I listen to the sound our lips make, teasing, biting.

"Do you remember what you wrote me?" She moves on top of me. My lungs constrict as electric pulses weave up my legs. "When I left?"

"What was it?"

"Think back . . . like that . . . just like that . . ."

I exhale and stare into her face and I try.

"I can always tell the first day of spring." Lisa's reading from her notebook as cold rain blows against the windows. We talked earlier about how glad we were it wasn't snow. "The air is heavy, but not weighted, and the robin's dewy melody careens through the houses and trees. The smell, too—the captive smells of life are released from the thawing ground. The rising mist is thicker than fog. Open a window and taste its essence, put a hand through and feel. It's the senses that tell you when the seasons shift, and the first day of spring is the most sensual day of the year."

"Wonderful, Lisa," I say. "You're following the prompt exactly right. Can you tell me what the prompt is again?"

She flips through her pages, stops at a paragraph from a few weeks ago. "*Using the most intricate detail, describe a memory, and tie it to a season. Use sensual imagery from the season to deepen the memory, to the point you can recall it after reading it.*"

"That is fabulous, Lisa," Darren says, eyes closed. His mouth hangs open, and I wish it wasn't sleeting so he could taste March through an open window. "I've always considered the first day of summer the most sensual, but you may have changed my mind."

"First day of summer?" I ask. "Why?"

"I'm not sure I can remember, but . . ." he leans forward and rubs his temples, "but I remember the smell the exhaust from the semis would make in June—maybe it was hot rubber burning on hot asphalt as the sun was setting on Friday nights, getting out of the shop."

Sam walks in, limping. "Sorry, gang. I forgot."

On the ride back into the city, I think about what Sam told me after we finished—the project he wants to do for the compilation journal I'm putting together for the end of our session. I get over to the far-right lane and move with the slow traffic to concentrate. He said he's been thinking of fall—of September, the month he was married and the month his daughter was born. He wants to articulate that the changing colors of leaves—green to red, yellow, brown—is not decay but a visible metamorphosis. It makes me think of her, how what we do together is so dangerous because of the chasm it opens in me again—in us. I know we loved each other with primal fierceness, and I remember how long I felt hollowed when she left. I can't make sense of what has changed in us, between us; and the way we are remembering each other through our senses makes me lose track of the time that ticks by, silent and unnoticed.

. . .

We sit at opposite ends of the bed.

"When did you know I was leaving?" she asks.

"Why do you want to know?"

"I never wanted to . . . I didn't think . . . just tell me."

"When we lived together that winter. One night, trains woke me up from a nightmare, a life without you, but the trains pulled me from that life and thrust me back into bed, where you were draped over my chest, trying to push me away. Your fingers were calloused."

"From working at that salon on Hilton Road." She leans forward, away from me. "Saving money for Minneapolis, before I knew I was leaving. The salon's closed now—I tried calling the other day." She rolls over onto her stomach and lifts her feet in the air, moves them back and forth. "I remember sitting up nights by your windowsill before I left you; how I heard the engines first pulling along the rusty tracks, then the bells of the crossing station before the whistles blew and all other sound was cancelled, gone. In that moment when the noise rushed by, I would close my eyes and I wasn't there, not in Ferndale, not in your bedroom . . . I watched you, wrapped in your white sheets, your skin forgetting its summer tan, calling me back to do what we had always done so well together."

I'm soaked in that memory, wet with it.

"I never wanted to break your heart." She wraps me in her arms and kisses the sunken place behind my collarbone.

"You need to tell me why you left."

I run to the party store on the corner of Second and Prentis to get something to drink. I don't think I'm ready to hear her answer, and I want to be numbed when I do. I buy a pint of whiskey and pause before the mural. I sip and cough and look at the cars: the sharp lines of a Cadillac DeVille, the muscled snarl of a Plymouth Barracuda. They were made here, I think to myself, hand after hand on metal.

. . .

We watch the red flashing lights from the Windsor casino silently dance on the surface of the river.

"When Dynamic closed, we had to leave," she says. "You couldn't. I did."

"We could have made it work."

"It would have gotten harder and harder. We would have resented each other by the end of it—the steady erosion of possibilities. And I had to see what a life without you, without Detroit, would be like."

"So was it a compulsion?"

"No . . ."

"Then you didn't have to. No one has to do anything."

"It became . . ." she turns over and her hair falls on my chest, "it became sustenance, you know? It became something I needed to sustain me. It's so hard to live here—you know that. I needed love to live here. I needed it like food, like water . . ." She looks me in the eye. "That shouldn't be the only reason. That's not what love is. That's not what love should be, I don't think—I didn't think."

The red lights flash above her head.

"Light comes in through the window earlier now. I tilt the blinds so the light hits my eyes and wakes me up." Lisa's reading her piece to the group. She says it's nearly done; at least, she thinks so.

"I can't say that brings me much joy here," Sam interrupts, though not on purpose. "My damn blinds don't work. I'm awake by eight, whether I want to be or not." I look at Sam and realize I want to know him more, that maybe he'll open up to me and the group through his work, but it's hard without his family here to fill in the blanks of his past.

"Go on, Lisa," I say.

"I think this light, for me, is the love of my family that I've forgotten. Something that remains in a suspended form. It exists independently of my dying brain, manifesting itself in the eyes of my husband and children. In their words I can hear but don't understand. In the way they touch my arm. In the fragrance that emerges from the apple pie they bring me, which they tell me was my favorite, is my favorite, and when I taste it

I am transformed by this transubstantiated love, and for a moment it is spring in my mind." Lisa stops and looks at me. "Do you like it?"

I realize I'm wearing a sad expression. "Very much. I just don't like talking about death and love at this time of year for some reason."

"What do you think about death?" Lisa asks me. "I'm curious how someone as young as yourself would feel about it. Being so far away."

"I think . . ." I pause and look out the window, at the melting snow, "to think of death, I have to think of life—of the act of creation. I think of sex as the ultimate sensual experience and death as the obliteration of the senses. Lisa, if you remember, the opening of your piece deals with the most sensual day of the year for you. For me, death would be an inability to interpret, to appreciate that day through the denial of taste, of touch . . ." I see that they have all closed their eyes, stopped talking.

A minute goes by. Darren flips through his notebook, making silent corrections.

Sam clears his throat. "I'm starting to remember something."

"Good," I say, flipping to a new page.

"Well, it's fall, the early fall . . ."

The drive down I-75 is better in March. Februarys are existential, brutal. There's an absence of sense about February—the shortest month that feels the longest, the longest days of winter that feel the shortest, the warmest nights that feel the coldest. There's a blandness, too—in dusk on the freeway everything looks the same, the colors from the other cars diluted by dirty snow, everything a mulled gray. The heater in the car turns smell into a fumy nothing, the Styrofoam cup turning coffee into flavorless heat. For some reason, I can always remember the first day of winter because of February jaunts down I-75—I can see the death of fall, when the sensual world retreats. I never have Darren or Lisa or Sam write about this because it almost cripples me with sadness, though for another reason, too, that I don't want to recall.

"Why do you work up there if you live down here in the Cass Corridor?" She's in the bathroom brushing her teeth.

"It's hard to say." I'm in bed, the right side of the mattress starting to remember the curve of my back.

"You don't remember?"

I feel the heaviness in my chest that I get when I lie—guilt from a lapsed Catholic. "I think it's because it's so close to . . ."

"Where we lived, right?"

"Yeah, right by Dynamic." To tell her I became a facilitator to channel my grief, to help others with fleeting memory would give too much away—I'm not ready. "Still, when I left, it scared me. All the padlocked factories and vacant storefronts, the foreclosed homes." I tilt my head and watch her brush. "It was like living in . . ."

"A graveyard?" She spits and looks at me through the bathroom mirror.

"Yeah." I see her eyes and smile. "Come here."

"It's like I was trying to forget something . . . for a long time, forgetting something that was already gone."

She pins me on my back.

"After a while, it was like I was looking for something . . ."

"That no longer exists." She kisses me and I can taste the mint of her toothpaste. "My dad talks about it when he's drunk at our cottage. How much he misses it, you know, picking pallet splinters out of his coffee every morning, the monotonous clang of the work bell. Riotous Friday nights in seedy bars, betting entire paychecks on darts, on pool, on shuffleboard. Sunday Mass and confirmations, beer league softball in the summer months. The long, fuzzy Memorial Days, Fourth of Julys, Labor Days on forgotten inland lakes. That was the poem I couldn't finish after I left. But how do you describe that? How do you describe the evaporation? It's too saccharine, inauthentic."

I pull her head up and kiss her again, move my tongue over her smooth white teeth. "But the people up there, at American House, they remember . . ."

"Are you lonely, son?" Sam asks me this during our break.

"I was for a few years," I tell him. "Not right now."

"One of the nurses asked me if I was lonely today. I said, 'No, I'm not lonely. I've never felt lonely. You'll always have your memories.'"

I think about telling him that his daughter visits every day, but then Darren and Lisa walk back into the room, take their seats.

We have an hour of free writing before they finish their final projects. Afterward, they share their pieces, laughing as they critique each other. Lisa, the last to leave, takes my hand and says, "I don't know what your name is, but you are a wonderful facilitator. I really look forward to working with you."

The mural's been worked on—I can see details in the visage of the workers and their children. I study the faces and wonder if they know the violence that's coming, if they are conscious that the buildings will burn, that their grandchildren will pick out a wall on the deserted part of a deserted street and try to resuscitate something that exists like a scar on the face of the young.

"I got the job," she says. We're sitting on the cracked windowsill watching steam rise from manhole covers.

"At the place down the street?"

"Yeah. It's part-time, but at least I can keep a schedule. Helps with writing."

"Have you done any since you've been back?"

She shakes her head, taps her fingers on the window.

"You need some inspiration?" I smile and walk to the bedside table.

"What's that?" she asks as I bring the folded paper back to the window.

> I can picture
> you: dark-haired, shaded
> blue-black with night;
> it seemed when we fell in love to be silk
> I ran between my fingers.
> You grew out your winter color, laughing
> as the roots turned light.
> Me, keen observer of how
> you wore it: up when working, braids for

parties, down around your shoulders
when it was us alone.

It's cut off now, your friends said.
Sleeker, without affection
that someone else will stroke.

As I read, I know I must have written it when we she left, but afterward
when we embrace, all I can hear is the rhythm our bodies make as we
consume each other again and again, the pitch of our groans, and the rigid
tonality of my cheap bed. The physical is easy for us, trying to fit into
each other's lives, again, only to slip away, exhausted.

As my words fade through my, *our* cracked window, the thought of
cracking myself open to welcome something permanent is terrifying. I
know I'm just a cracked façade, and as we kiss, I hope it excavates the
buried memories of our dead life together to move me beyond this stage
of benign and postured lust.

The home sent the manuscripts down Woodward Heights to a printing
place off Hilton Road. They made copies for every participant and every
member of their immediate families. We don't title it, and the cover
photograph, of the train tracks on Nine Mile and Hilton stretching all the
way down to the river, lights from the night shift at Dynamic Fabricating illuminating the dusk, that Darren took when he was young and his
children brought to me when our session began, seems more appropriate
than anything we could think of.

The families gather in the room, hold their elders' shaky hands. After
we're settled, I look over at Sam. I can tell he doesn't recognize me
because of the motion of his eyes.

"Thank you, families," I say, "for joining us today for the anthology
reading. Since he's been waiting to share this lyric essay since our class
began, I'd like to begin with Sam. Sam, would you like to read, or should I?"

He looks over at his daughter, who squeezes his hand. "I'll read," he
says, "if you could introduce it."

"Sam has titled this piece, 'Green September.'"

He takes a deep breath, looks at his piece in the journal for the first time. When he's finished and I remind him that he's written this exquisite, unique thing, I like to think he will remember, however briefly, every memory he transferred from his mind to the page, where they will live through other eyes as long as they remain open.

Sam clears his throat. The expectant eyes of the room are on him. I won't tell them that I will return next month in the florid bloom of spring to begin another class with them and that they may not remember me, or the journal, or this moment when their memories became text.

"From my room, far away, I watch us play. Years later, I watch us pull open the fence and crawl under, our scabbed knees opening again. Though I am old and I am dying, we are still young—always young, our hair and eyes bright as we weave through concrete mazes, breathe the carbon in the air.

"We always play the same game—four square, at the intersection of four concrete slabs—in the same place. Back then it was the only shop closed, the property 'cursed'—the only one vacant among humming dozens.

"But it's magical. Engines roar around us, smoke sighs from chimneys, and the last breath of summer fades on the lips of the wind. We play until dark, until the engines go quiet and the leaves begin to fall in the cool night breeze."

He pauses, unsure again of his work, surprised by its elegance. Maybe if he creates this memory, he can attach it to this moment and then, maybe, he can remember the people he once loved.

"Now everything is closed—all the shops have rusty fences and For Lease signs faded from long days in the summer sun. But if I look—if I really look, if I narrow my eyes and focus, I can see us playing in the ruins, playing in defiance, in defense of the last green of September before the nights get long."

The room takes a breath, then Sam continues.

• • •

It's a gorgeous night in Detroit—the kind of balmy March evening that makes everyone knock on wood, lets them believe, however briefly, that the worst is over. And as I park my car on Willis, I think that this is what Alzheimer's would be like for me, if it robbed me not only of my memory, but the control of my memory—it would be a warm, clear March night that winter has not yet left, lingering to pull at my senses.

I hold the journal in my hand, feel the weight of it, the way Darren and Lisa and Sam say I should feel the weight of the Bible, its mass, as I turn the corner onto Cass and stop.

The wall is empty, blasted clean with white paint. The mural has disappeared. I close my eyes and try to recreate it; open them and project its memory on the concrete wall.

I look down the street and she's there in the window, and I remember what I love about her, not the material, the base, the physical, the sensual, but her capacity for love, how she can express it without effort. What a coward I've been.

I run my hand across the barrenness and walk home.

At home, we read the journal together.

"When does the next session start?" she asks.

"In the spring," I say, eyes lingering on Lisa's piece.

She turns my face toward hers, meets my eyes. "Do you need any help?"

"I think they'd love you."

She closes the book and puts her head on my chest, my muscles starting to remember its shape. "Alex?" It's the second time she's said my name.

"Yes, Delia?" The second time I've said hers.

"Do you remember when I came back to you? When I asked about what you wrote for me when I left?"

I stroke her hair and notice its coarseness, how the strands stick to the damp spaces between my fingers lathered in her sweat.

"I forgot it." And here's the moment, now, when I can fall back into her.

"You didn't." She moves away from me, searches through her luggage for a yellowed envelope. She opens it, faces the wall. "I know you didn't."

I met you in the death of fall;
the days were curt and so were you.
Pensive, sitting across from me
in empty bars;
jokes with straight faces;
we were coy.

I fell in love in the dead of winter;
the nights were long and so were ours.
No clocks, time a concept; we got familiar
with each other
again and again;
we were trying.

Spring came, the snow thawed;
the days were warm and so were we.
We emerged from our hibernation
then doubled back, scared without
constraints;
we were hiding.

Summer came, lush and green;
the days were long and so were ours.
Your hands grew softer with sweat, skin
darker from sun
as we chased sunsets;
we were running.

Fall came with wind and leaves;
the days grew cold and so did we.

We held each other
saying nothing
but that we would never leave;
we were lying.

You left me in the death of fall;
one year,
it must have been.
And alone I felt the slow
death of a love which
was born, after all, in the death of fall.

She stands up and walks over to the window. She opens the curtains and looks across the ruins of the city, the shells of what was returning to dust.

"It was gorgeous." She leans her head against the glass. "Wasn't it?"

Warm air sifts through the blinds, then all is silent.

CANDY

Lorca's Tortas

There were three of them: a heavyset guy with a scraggly beard and garish tattoos, a slim guy with a tapered haircut and beautifully crafted scowl, and a sleekly dressed woman with sharply angled red bangs. They all looked younger than me—early twenties, I guessed. They stood outside in the florid spring night air, checking the engine of my ice cream truck, walking through the interior.

"This," the woman said to herself, "is the start of something big."

"What are your plans for it?" I asked. "If you don't mind me asking."

"Food truck," said the bearded one. "New concept. Artisanal sandwiches for common working folks."

There wasn't much work around the neighborhood, but I swallowed my bitterness. "Well, I hope it brings you more luck than it brought me."

The woman leaned her checkbook on her leg and signed for the full amount. "We've all been wanting to do this for a while—ever since we graduated college. Isn't that right, fellas?"

The slim guy lit a cigarette. "It'll be nice having something to do every day. I've been bored out of my mind in Ann Arbor."

"So, you guys are Michigan grads?" I asked.

"Yes," said the woman, handing me the check. "We've been looking for the opportunity to create a positive social, political, and economic project for the Detroit region—it was my senior thesis."

The woman perched in the driver's seat, motioned to me in the side window. "By the way—can you work a knife?"

"A little, I guess."

"Prep work, I mean—maybe some face-to-face interaction?"

"I think I'm open to anything at this point." No one had yet asked me why I was selling.

"But you're good with people?"

"Kids and old people. Not too good with the ones my own age."

"Just the demographics we need some help attracting!"

"Are you offering me a job?"

"Well, I figured you could use one."

I wanted to cry but didn't see the point. I just thought Camus was full of shit. There was no such thing as rebellion in purgatory. I stuck out my hand.

"I'm Roxy," she said, shaking it. "The big one is Doug, and the small one is Harper."

"I'm Candice," I said, waving to my new colleagues. "My friends call me Candy."

"Candy," said Harper. "That's a sweet name."

Candy. It didn't sound as cute rolling off a grown man's lips.

One year earlier, I had stopped by John K. King Books on Woodward after putting my severance check from the community center in the bank. As an avid reader who now found herself with a lot of time on her hands, I figured I'd stock up before the spring rains came to blanket the city. The secretary from the community center used to give me weathered copies of Bukowski, Carver, Yates, telling me they were cushions to sit on a hard world with. But I never understood their fear of the American suburbs, a sucking existential vacuum turning you into some hopeless, unfeeling, expendable good. My neighborhood always sang to me, a siren's song calling through the train whistles and diesel engines, the auction signs and repo vans, the space stretched out like dough with only leafy trees keeping your dreams pinned down. That's why I love April, early spring: the naked trees ringed with throbbing bulbs, ready to bloom and suffocate foolish dreams of escape. What is there to escape, after all? What is there to dream? I believe what my favorite existentialists believed: that all of us will pass from this big fake world that churns us through its economic gears. And in my dreams, I'm in those empty streets of the east side of Ferndale, home to former factories and their former workers, and I'm licking vanilla ice cream from my fingers as the truck's nursery rhyme music chimes away, hoping that dream will be my eternal one.

Under the fluorescent lights, I perused the aisles of dark wood shelves for a weathered copy of *The Myth of Sisyphus*, looking to replace the one I'd given my best friend Suzanne when she left for Hollywood after high school, determined to make the definitive movie about Detroit. In his book, Camus muses on the absurdity of existing in an indifferent universe without any defined meaning. He comes up with three solutions: suicide (simple enough to define), delusion (either blissful ignorance or the cynical return to religion), or rebellion (embracing the absurd, as the individual strives to create their own meaning). In Sisyphus, the Greek king forced by the gods to eternally push a rock up a hill, Camus finds a perfect blend of all three. And as I lingered at the register, playing with that deposit slip in my pocket, *I* mused on those choices, now starkly real.

Suicide.

Delusion.

Rebellion.

So what did I do with that check?

After the feds took a quarter off the top and I paid off my credit cards?

After my colleagues moved on to recreation programs farther up on Woodward that still had money, Birmingham and Rochester and Bloomfield Hills, or left for Teach for America in New Orleans, or went back to being counselors at their old summer camps up north?

After I spent two months canvassing the area with résumés, looking for something that could pay me to stay?

I did what every sane person would do: I bought an ice cream truck and filled it with all my favorite stuff: ice cream sandwiches and Creamsicles and King Cones. I rebelled.

I figured I could capitalize on that entrepreneurial spirit that infects Detroit—or used to, at least. And nothing personifies it better than an ice cream truck. Taking a form of transportation created by our proud local industry and creating a delivery service that brings small consumable pleasures to the young, the hopeful. Few other occupations, I thought, could be so rewarding.

Everyone wants to be their own boss; it's the American Dream. And that's what I painted on the side: The American S'Cream.

My parents thought I was crazy—*stupid*, was what my dad said. They had taken their (far more generous) buyouts—from Chrysler and the Ferndale Public schools—and bought a double-wide on Lake Huron, giving me the keys to my childhood house, telling me to hawk it when the business failed. I told them that just because their dreams hadn't come true—if they even had any to begin with—that didn't mean mine would fail.

And so, on the first day of April, I loaded up the truck and set off around the east side of Ferndale, making sure to stop in front of every house of the kids from the community center. *Welcome to the service economy, east side*, I thought to myself. *You may not like it, you may not want it, but I'm going bring it to you in a way you can digest and enjoy.*

When I drove the truck over to my grandpa's house to take him on one of our weekday field trips to watch his beloved Tigers on TV, he let out a smoker's laugh and walked up to the service window.

"Gimme a Firecracker," he said.

I helped him into the passenger seat. I drove us to Kady's Bar, and we had afternoon beers with the other Dynamic Fabricating retirees, swapping tales about life on the shop floor or vignettes about their late wives.

"I ever tell you about the time your grandmother tried to talk me in to buying a roadside ice cream stand up north, in Gladwin?" my grandpa asked me.

He had, but it was one of my favorite stories. "Refresh my memory."

"We used to drive past it every summer on our way to the cottage—when your mother was just a kid. Every year it got more and more decrepit, paint chipping off, lettering on the sign more and more unreadable. Every time, your grandmother would tug at my sleeve from the passenger seat, saying, 'This year? It doesn't need much.' She would handle the front; I'd mix the soft serve. A working retirement." He paused, sipped his beer. "Your grandmother," he finally said. "She was a hell of a woman."

"That she was." On the TV the rain lifted, the grounds crew removing the infield tarp in Cleveland.

I looked out the back door. In the parking lot, kids gathered around the truck, and I spotted a few I knew from the center, a few loose bills in their pockets, holding written directions from their parents to stay out of trouble.

"You got the right idea with this thing, Candy," he said. "At least you won't have to take shit all day like the fuckers in here did." He leaned forward and raised his glass toward the grizzled afternoon drinking crowd. "Drink up, you bastards. For my granddaughter. For good luck."

They raised their glasses, clinked them together. I raised mine, downed it, and made my way toward the back door.

My grandpa put a hand on my shoulder. "I mean this, sweetheart—I think this could be the start of something big for you."

That's what I thought, too: that it would be a smashing success, that I would be so busy that it would start to eat into my productivity, that my market share would grow too large and that I would have to buy more trucks and hire more people, all while staying in touch with and continuing to tutor, as much as I could, the kids from the center.

But it didn't happen. After breaking even that spring, the kids came up to the truck and waved sadly, giving me the change they found in their sofas or under their beds. I told them their money wasn't any good, had them play I spy or race them across the street and back. It wasn't as fun as playing capture the flag in the dead of winter, using the administrative office as the safe zone, and it wasn't as fun as playing human Sorry! in the rec room, using Slip 'N Slides to knock people off a huge parchment board. But it brought us all together, again, and it gave me time to tell them, again, that they could do whatever they wanted, as long as it was something they loved.

But soon the kids ran out of change for the ice cream, and their parents ran out of money for their mortgage, and one by one they were all replaced on their front lawns by foreclosure signs as they moved north to shack up with their extended families. Soon it was just me and the birds flying back from Florida with the retired folks on their pensions (the lucky bastards), both flocks glaring and cawing at me as they fixed their tattered nests.

I swallowed my pride, called around to my former coworkers from the community center. Some told me to learn a skilled trade—coding or massage therapy—some told me to go to grad school—using government loans to pay my bills—some told me to remember something I loved as a kid—writing or painting or music—and join them in the big cities, going back into the real world when it was feasible again.

From my vantage point in the driver's seat, I watched the seasons change: spring to summer, summer to fall, until I finally locked American S'Cream up in my grandpa's garage for the winter.

And it was May of the next year when I finally ran through my severance and my savings, when I realized the futility of my own rebellion and put the truck up for sale on Craigslist.

Oh well, I thought. Maybe I could donate the rest of the ice cream. I was eating the last of the Firecrackers with my grandpa on his front porch, listening to the Tigers broadcast on the radio when my phone rang, someone responding to the ad.

"Is this Candice?" asked the high-pitched voice on the other line.

"You can call me Candy. I don't have any use for formalities now."

"OK—Candy, just a few quick questions. Does it have room for a kitchen inside?"

I told her the dimensions through my brain freeze.

"Perfect, just perfect. Can we come take a look tonight?"

"I'm not going anywhere." I told her the address and we hung up.

"Well, that sounds like good news," my grandpa said, unwrapping another Popsicle.

"It was delusional, wasn't it?" I asked. On the radio, our closer loaded the bases. "It was delusional to think this would work."

"You did your best."

Fuck Camus, I thought. "Maybe it was suicidal."

.   .   .

The business was named after Federico García Lorca, the Spanish poet murdered by the fascists during their civil war, whose gorgeously textured laments were my companions during the long winter nights in college. Roxy wanted to operate the company in his spirit, said that the value of the "brand" was unique, that it wasn't so much a business as an anarcho-syndicalist collective operating in a market economy, "like the Catalan Republic in the 1930s."

We had five different tortas, all created by Doug: Classic (beans, queso fresco, lettuce, tomatoes, hot sauce) Greek (Gyro meat, tomato, onion, tzatziki), Italian (salami, provolone, olive tapenade, vinaigrette), American (brisket, American cheese, caramelized onions, barbeque sauce), and Asian (chicken, cabbage, carrots, teriyaki glaze). Each one was designed to be the most popular depending on what Detroit neighborhood Harper picked during his mid-morning brood: Mexicantown, Greektown, Eastern Market, the Cass Corridor, Lafayette Park. Roxy always had a copy of the *Metro Times* handy to look for weekend excursions to music festivals or trade shows. Roxy said she wanted to generate as much hype as quickly as possible so we could start grabbing lucrative catering gigs for the summer, which was rapidly approaching.

It took a single week for the four of us to transform American S'Cream into Lorca's Tortas. Doug drove the truck to a kitchen supply wholesaler and had it refitted with a flattop, a grease trap, and compact essentials for him to "execute his vision," as he put it. Roxy drove it to Somerset Collection and bought two high-end iPads with credit card readers, which she demonstrated to me with ease. Harper drove it to Home Depot and picked out the most expensive black, red, and yellow paint they had. He had painted houses during summer breaks in college, "Not 'cause I had to," he said, "but more to get some sun, stay in shape," and so relished the opportunity to craft a mixed Catalan and anarcho-syndicalist flag design over the white, pink, and baby blue façade I loved so much. As for me, I spent most of the time in my grandpa's kitchen, trying my best to emulate YouTube videos of proper slicing techniques with my grandma's dull cooking knives.

Although there were no official job titles (in keeping with Lorca's

Tortas' anarchist ethos), the four of us fell in as such: Roxy was the face of the company, in charge of social media and drumming up hype in the food blogs and the immediate areas where we decided to park and serve. Doug was the executive chef, in charge of the menu and procuring our wares from the sprawling Eastern Market in downtown Detroit every morning. In baseball parlance, I was a "utility" player, prepping the vegetables, working the register, walking the street corners to pass out flyers. As for Harper, I wasn't sure what he did besides be condescending toward Doug and me while gazing longingly at Roxy. He mentioned something about being the "numbers guy," but Roxy trained only me to work the mobile register, only me to crunch the credit card receipts for the end of a shift.

On the day of our soft open, a cloudless May beauty, we drove the truck to Campus Martius in downtown Detroit—a small, U-shaped patch of green at the intersection of Woodward and Michigan Avenue lined with trees and pavilions that filled with lunching office workers in the warmer months. I uncovered the meats and vegetables, looking up at the skyscrapers that ringed the park. When Roxy confidently stuck our permit on the service window, I caught a glimpse of the gorgeously intricate tattoo sleeve adorning her left arm: a long Spanish poem gracefully following the billows of a red and yellow Catalan flag.

"What does it say?" I asked her as I arranged the containers.

She planted her foot on the tailgate, looked off into the distance, and recited "Lament for the Death of a Bullfighter." "My favorite Lorca poem," she said with a flourish. "My favorite poem period, honestly."

After two hours of prep work, Roxy brought out a large portable chalkboard and wrote down the menu. At noon, workers from the surrounding office buildings poured out into the park, many making a beeline to the truck.

Roxy grabbed a loudspeaker. "Welcome, Detroit, to a culinary revolution! Five of the most delicious sandwiches you'll ever eat, constructed with the grace of poetry and labor of true solidarity!"

Our first customers ordered more out of curiosity than anything else, asking for half portions so they could sample the entire menu. But they *were* delicious—something I could easily attest to—and so they ordered more to take back inside for their coworkers, who, minutes later, returned to clean us out.

Although it took a while for me to get used to, the routine wasn't awful: I began driving to Eastern Market every morning with Doug to buy the ingredients at 7 a.m., the same time I used to unlock the community center during our summer program to plan the activities and stock the fridge with juice boxes and cold cut sandwiches. After that, it was prep work in Doug's West Village kitchen before loading up the truck and heading into Detroit for the lunch crowd.

The week after our grand opening, I got to Doug's early—we were hitting a parking lot in Greektown during a Tigers day game, and after the unexpected success of our opening, we were anticipating a large crowd.

"You must be happy," I said as I washed tomatoes in his sink.

"Why would I be happy?"

"After last week. We sold out of everything. It's your menu. You must be proud, right?"

Doug let out a weighted breath, held a block of aged cheddar to a shiny cheese grater. "It's flattering. That's for sure."

"Don't be so modest," I said. "It must feel fulfilling to create something so many people enjoy."

He paused, stared at the fallen shreds in a plastic container. "You think Rox did?"

"What?"

"The tortas. You think she liked them?"

"I don't see why that matters."

"Really?"

"It's a business, Doug. Why do you care if the people you're in business with think your product is good? That's for the consumers to decide."

"It's complicated." He grated harder, the shreds becoming thicker.

"Not really. I'm telling you from experience. It's all about bringing a popular product to an expanding market."

He stopped grating again, stared out of the window above the kitchen sink, and I thought, finally, one of them will ask about *my* business, how much I loved it, how it had failed. "I'm not unattractive, right, Candy?"

"I'm sorry?"

"I know I'm bigger than most guys, but I have a lot to offer, don't I? Like you said—I'm a good cook at least, right?"

I started nervously slicing the tomatoes. "Yeah—a great cook."

"Harper's just . . . is it 'cause he's thinner than I am? Nastier?"

My mind flipped back to the day they bought the truck—the exchange of fleeting glances as they examined the tomb of my ambition. "These are done," I said, transferring the tomatoes into a container and covering them with Saran Wrap.

The day went fantastic, another sellout replete with hashtagged posts on social media building upon our growing word-of-mouth buzz. My grandpa took a bus in from Kady's with some other Dynamic retirees, and I met him in an adjacent parking lot after the game was over.

"You guys really should park the truck in front of the ballpark for every afternoon game," he said. We leaned against the bus, and I cracked a beer for each of us, watching a steady stream of fans—dressed in white jerseys and blue caps emblazoned with the Tigers' famous English *D*—look for cover from the pounding midday sun. "You'd make a killing."

"I suggested it," I said, sliding my beer into a koozie. "They don't seem too interested in my ideas, unfortunately."

"They don't know what they're talking about."

I tilted my head back, felt the heat bake my face. "Maybe I should get another job. I just don't know what else I'd be good at."

"Well, if Dynamic were still open, I'd get you in there."

"I wouldn't mind. All I heard in high school was how boring and repetitive manufacturing work was—and how there was intrinsic, material value in reading the great works of literature. But you never hated Dynamic, right?"

"Are you kidding? All the time."

"But work is work, right?" He would always tell me that when my parents brought me over to his house to mow the lawn and collect empty beer cans when I was a kid.

"Listen. At Kady's, most of what you hear is nostalgia. The bullshit gets left behind. But this is the God's honest truth: at some point—and some people realize this quicker than others—you realize that you're busting your ass to make someone else rich."

"I never knew you were Red, grandpa."

"But after you accept that, it's sort of, I don't know, liberating? We got paid decent, Candy—that's the big difference between then and now. Pay is shit now." He lifted his beer, motioned across the street to the food truck. "How much they paying you?"

"Nine dollars an hour."

"Nine dollars an hour—shit pay, Candy. But easier work, right? More variety?"

For the first time, I asked myself: *Would* I have wanted a job like my grandpa's? Getting up with the sun and smelling the polluted morning? Would I have loved that commute down Hilton Road on my bike, have loved to churn out those machining contracts on the floor with everybody, bitching about the incompetency of management during breakfast and lunch breaks? Would I have loved to have the financial security to marry and pop out some kids and buy a bungalow within walking distance of the parks for us to laugh and swear and eat and drink on Sundays after Mass—all of that, if I could?

"Anyways, it's gone, dear." He finished his beer and surveyed the vacant buildings on the edge of downtown. "Maybe it's for the best. Nothing lasts forever. Someone's gotta do *something* with those buildings."

The next week, waiting for lunch rush on the leafy corner of Woodward and Kirby, Roxy skipped up to the truck, carrying a copy of the latest *Metro Times*.

"Ahem," she said, theatrically clearing her throat. "*Hats off to Lorca's Tortas, an innovative food truck currently doing the lunch rounds in the city's hippest up-and-coming neighborhoods.*"

Doug poked his head through the service window. "What does it say about the menu?"

"*Chef Doug LaFleur's eclectic menu is sure to satisfy even the most discerning foodie.*" She winked at Doug, then looked back down to the paper. "*It has something for just about everyone.*"

Smoking near the back door, even Harper cracked a smile. "We should go get more copies." He flicked his cigarette into the street and looked across Woodward to the retirees and school kids milling around the bronze replica of Rodin's *The Thinker.* "Hand them out to the art snobs."

We . . . well, *I* did. The museum patrons mentioned they'd already heard the buzz, and after the museum workers saw them eating our tortas on the museum's front lawn, instead of complaining, ordered dozens of them for the docents, the cashiers, the baristas. We sold out before 1:00 p.m.

Afterward, we went to a new bar in Hazel Park to celebrate—some kind of ironic tiki lounge with fifteen dollar mai tais.

"First round's on me," Harper said, pulling out a platinum American Express. "Something sweet for you, Candy?" He winked.

"I'll have a Stroh's bottle and a shot of Jameson," I said, looking around at the burning torches, the faux-grass umbrellas that covered the patio.

"How old fashioned."

"Not sure what that means," I took the shot, "but thanks for the drinks."

"Tell me about yourself," he said as he scoped the bar for other girls. "You weren't that talkative on our trips to Home Depot."

"You never asked."

He sprouted a prideful grin. "I guess I was too excited about the business."

I sighed. "What do you want to know?"

"Oh, I dunno . . . likes, dislikes, you know the drill."

"Why now?" I asked.

He glanced in the direction of Roxy, who was flirting with the bartender, a mirror image of Harper with a newer haircut and a longer torso. "No one else to talk to."

"Thanks for the honesty." I took a swig of my beer. "I like kids, community . . . as an idea and reality . . . ice cream, watching baseball games with my grandpa . . ."

Harper didn't even wait till I finished. "Dislikes?"

I took another swig. "The lack of opportunity here. Camus's thesis on absurdity. The fact that I . . ."

"Lack of opportunity?" Harper downed his mai tai, ordered another. "The fuck are you talking about? It's like a blank slate here. Everything's up for grabs."

"Where did you grow up?"

"If I say Bloomfield Hills, will you judge me?"

"Of course I will."

"Why?"

I sipped my beer and thought about trying to articulate my conversation with my grandpa at the Tigers' game to Harper, but when I collected my thoughts and looked over, Harper was flipping through the lighted screen of his smartphone, his eyes glazed and distant.

"That's why," I finally said. "Pretending to care."

Harper looked at Roxy, who was tracing the outlines of the bartender's tattoos with her fingers, then leaned forward and looked at me. "Sorry," he said. "I get easily distracted. I have ADHD . . . at least I did when I was growing up."

"Some of my kids did, too."

Harper ordered another mai tai, sipped it angrily. "You have kids?"

"Not my own. From the community center I used to work at. That's why I bought the truck."

"To stay in touch with them?"

I nodded, stared out onto the patio.

"That's pretty cool, actually."

"Thanks."

"I'm sorry it didn't work out," he said.

"That's life."

"I can relate, actually."

He bowed his head, looked at Roxy, then back at me.

Roxy danced over to us, holding up her phone.

"What are you so happy about?" Harper said.

"It must be the *Metro Times* piece, but we just got our first catering gig! This Sunday!"

"No shit?" asked Doug, walking over with a plate of Spam musubi.

"It's a tent revival in Ferndale—right by where you live, Candy."

"What the fuck is a tent revival?" asked Harper.

I thought about telling them it was a traveling hucksterish Christian road show, but Roxy talked over me.

"Probably a carnival or something." Roxy hugged me, the light from the tiki torches illuminating the text on her arm. "Can you believe it, Candy? It's happening!"

I made dinner for my grandpa the next night, telling him about the good news. He told me that the truck I had chosen was lucky, and that although the luck was rubbing off on another business, I was still a part of it, in a small but important way. Afterward, I sat on the front porch and flipped through the itinerary for the catering gig. I pulled out my phone to text Doug about Eastern Market the next morning, then saw a voicemail alert from an area code I didn't recognize.

"Candy? It's Suzanne. Just came across a *Metro Times* article online about a food truck called Lorca's Tortas and saw you working the kitchen. Sounds like you're famous now. Anyway, I'd love to hear from you—it's been way too long."

I called her back after my grandpa fell asleep. "I finally bought another copy of *The Myth of Sisyphus*," I said into the phone.

"Is it as good as you remember?"

"I don't know about *good*. It's a lot more depressing."

The last time I'd seen Suzanne was at Kady's during Thanksgiving, three years after Dynamic closed and the funding for the community center started to run dry. She was thin and tan, told me stories of moving up from production assistant gigs to writer's rooms, who was and wasn't an asshole in Hollywood. I couldn't recall why we'd lost touch, though I sensed, rightly or wrongly, that she'd developed an attitude, a snobbishness toward her friends from high school who didn't leave like she did.

"How are your coworkers?" she said. "They certainly look like they were well-cast for their parts."

"They're OK. The two guys are still in love with the girl, I think."

"That's awkward."

"You don't know the half of it."

"What about you? You seeing anyone?" Suzanne asked.

"Slim pickings here, I'm afraid."

"You try any of the apps out yet? It's easy to meet someone, at least."

"The people I've met seem to exhibit the sterling qualities of both lethargy and misogyny, honestly. They buy me round after round of well whiskey, stare off into space when I describe my love of Eastern Bloc writers, then text me one-word messages at two in the morning on Saturdays."

"Do you ever wonder if that's how our parents met? What if that was the initial attraction: taking someone's love by convincing them of a better life as part of a team rather than alone?"

"I don't mind being alone, actually," I said. "I'd rather be alone than with a stranger with a drinking problem."

"My dad used to tell me that everyone in Detroit has a drinking problem," Suzanne said. "Said it helped with the monotony, made the place look pretty."

"One of my coworkers does—Harper, the small one in the article picture," I told her. "Although I wonder if that's just another affectation. The extent that these sad black sheep of bourgeois families will go to appear authentically 'working class' is beyond my understanding."

"It's the same here, unfortunately. I think they think we find it attractive."

"Dating just seems so dishonest."

"I'm not sure if *dishonest* is the right word. Manipulative, maybe."

"And if you don't engage in it, you're left out of life here completely."

"Well, you're still Catholic, right?"

I laughed. "I haven't made up my mind. I have been thinking about the saints, though—dying for something abstract."

"Do you feel like a martyr staying home?"

"I don't know. Can you be a secular martyr?"

"Ask the revolutionaries on your food truck."

"I think they're all atheists."

I heard a snort on the other line. "Atheism is the faith of the privileged. It fits in perfectly as the religion of this economy."

"What do you mean?" I realized how much I missed Suzanne—brash, quick to argue, impervious to insecurity.

"I think a religion declaring this world as the only authentic one is a religion that negates and invalidates suffering. Having this world be the only one is great, if you can afford it."

"Well, what's the alternative?" I said.

"There are three alternatives, right?"

"Suicide, delusion, rebellion . . . don't remind me. The wound's still fresh."

"What are you talking about? Your business looks like a real smash."

"It's not mine . . ." I pulled the phone away from my ear, listened to the train whistles pulling nearer. "I'll tell you another time. What are you working on over there, anyway? You ever finish that screenplay?"

"Which one?"

"The one about . . . oh, what was it . . . all those kids scraping by in Detroit?"

"It's a TV pilot, now. I want a bigger canvas to deconstruct how people love in a society without money."

"You have the right setting."

"I don't have a pitch yet. It's more of a reaction to everything being made out here that I fucking hate."

"Such as?"

"All that ukulele-scored, love-is-the-new-religion bullshit. Talk about privilege. You can place all the value you want into 'love' after the rent's paid and the clothes are mended . . . if you get bored by your own excess and can afford to be condescending toward religious people."

"You won't believe what we're catering tomorrow."

"A job fair?"

"Close. A tent revival."

"That's amazing! I didn't know they still existed."

"I still remember the one we stopped at on the drive to Daytona senior year."

"My favorite memory of Chattanooga."

We laughed for a while, then went silent.

"Candy?"

"Suz?"

"It's great talking to you again. It's hard not having close friends out here." I heard wind cut through the line. "Every relationship seems . . . I dunno . . . transactional."

"Yeah," I said, as my screen flashed with texts from Roxy telling me to get to Doug's early to prep 150 premade Classic tortas. "I know what you mean."

The pavilion was full when we pulled up to the park and drove down the gravel road to begin service. As we unpacked under the shade of an aging oak tree, I squinted at the short person standing on a hastily assembled wooden platform, holding court over his congregation with a loudspeaker. He looked familiar.

"Everyone's lost their faith," the little man said. "Catholics, Presbyterians, Methodists, Baptists. And why? Money. Everyone thought money could replace God's love, and now that the money's gone, people just wander around like zombies . . . like the dispossessed. But God never left, and through His Son Jesus, we have access to it. Always."

"Oh my God," I said.

"You getting inspired?" asked Doug.

"No—that's Arnold Simmons. I went to high school with him."

I wished that they could have seen Arnold in high school: the local con guy, the guy that could get you weed on short notice if your parents were going out of town, the guy you wouldn't want to leave your girlfriend around. As far as I knew, he'd had a hard time finding purpose since graduation: tried to join the Great Lakes Coast Guard but his eyes were too bad, tried starting his own record label but couldn't find marketable talent, tried his hand at water restoration but his allergies flared up. Before he started whatever this was, I'd heard he was delivering pizzas for what was obviously an old mob front on John R in Hazel Park, the only open business sandwiched between padlocked fabricating shops.

His sermon lasted an hour. When it was over, he was met with rapturous applause and a cascading refrain of *amens*. He held them for one final rendition of "Amazing Grace," and then everyone made for the truck.

He recognized me immediately when he walked to the truck after shaking the hands of his congregation, sweat dripping from his forehead.

"Sorry we don't have any pizza tortas for you," I said jokingly.

"That how I found God, Candy." He wiped his forehead, reached for a bottled water on the service window. "No kidding: I delivered this one pie—extra cheese and anchovies, I'll never forget—to this half-burned house on the east side of Detroit, and this little old lady came out. She said, 'I can't pay you in money, this is all I have.' And she hugged me and said, 'I forgive you.' And that's where I found Him, on the steps of that rickety house, pie in hand."

Arnold handed over our payment from a wadded ball of money pulled from the inside pocket of his blazer, and one by one, his congregation walked up and received the premade sandwiches and brought them back to the pavilion.

After we washed up, I followed Arnold to his flock, chatting about who we went to high school with and what they were doing to make a living. Under the shaded canopy, everyone talked about the Second Coming, the End Times.

When everyone had finished eating, Arnold reached under our table and produced a briefcase. "That's the next part of the service," he said, bringing out a stack of papers and passing them around. It was a worksheet with a prompt that read: *A world without God and a world without work is a world without _____.*

"Meaning," said one person.

"Money," said another.

"Love," I said.

Arnold stared at me, shaking his head. "But there is love here. Love through God and His Son Jesus."

"If you say so," I said.

"You said so," said someone.

"I'm scared," said another. "I'm scared."

Arnold noticed many of them were bowing their heads. "What are you praying for?" he asked.

One after another, they said they'd gotten selfish, greedy, lazy; they had idolized work and money; and that God had deservedly exacted justice by taking their jobs away. They said they had complained about the hours, about being too tired, missing their families. They said they had griped about more overtime, more vacation days, more sick days. And God had listened and simply moved on.

I remembered what my parents told me about Catholicism before they moved up north: that it was just something people had to buy into while they worked crap jobs, and after they got money and passed it down to their kids it was just a relic—a set of ancient traditions and feasts to add some spice to the calendar year. It may or may not have been true—Camus would have filed it under delusion, I'm sure—but I was fairly certain that if my parents saw what was going to happen, when all that capital evaporated simultaneously with the means to acquire it, the real point of that faith would have been ravenously coveted, kept alive. What was I supposed to believe in now? A good laugh?

That's what Doug, Harper, and Roxy were doing as they packed up the food truck—laughing at the people hanging on Arnold's every word.

"I can't believe they believe that," Harper said.

Doug concurred. "How desperate can you be?"

Roxy smiled. "Take it easy. Christians buy tortas, too. Right, Candy?"

I laughed, a little. As a form of delusion, laughter wasn't bad.

Summer turned to fall as our pop-ups exclusively turned into gigs—just as Roxy had predicted. After catering a Labor Day party on Belle Isle, we went to another new bar on Eight Mile opened by one of Harper's high school friends. It was called Copper Wire, some kind of tribute to scrapping culture, with holes tastefully sledgehammered into freshly stuccoed walls, the new electrical work exposed for the customers to admire as they savored a Scrapyard—an herb-infused moonshine concoction that cost eighteen dollars.

I looked around at the rusted metal tables. "How much did it cost to renovate this place?" I asked the owner, a blond carbon copy of Harper whose eyes never moved from my chest.

"I'm not sure," he said. "I have a numbers guy for that."

"You know which bank gave you the loan? Comerica or something?"

He bristled, walked away.

"It was Father's Wallet, right?" Harper called after him. "Or Birmingham Trust?"

"That's a weird name for a bank," I said.

"It's a joke," sneered Harper. "His dad gave him the money. His dad's the numbers guy."

"Huh," I said. "Must have a good interest rate."

Harper sneered again. "You're such a dork."

"Thank you, Harper," I said.

"You need to lighten up," he said, taking another on-the-house shot. "Let me buy you a drink."

I put on my best fake smile. "Harper, when you were a kid, did you dream about growing up to be who you are? To treat people the way you do?"

"What are you talking about?"

I remembered what I used to patiently explain to my kids when they were acting out. "When you were a kid on the swing by yourself in the park after school, pumping your legs and trying to reach higher and higher until you could see over the tree line—were you dreaming about growing up to be cynical? Was that your ambition?"

"Whatever." He grabbed another shot and leered down the bar at Roxy, who was flirting with his blond look-alike. He sulked toward the pool table.

. . .

We drove the truck to West Village to drop off Doug and Harper, Roxy smoking in the driver's seat. "Candy," she said, "I feel bad about Harper. He shouldn't treat you like that."

"You don't have to apologize," I told her. "I know he doesn't."

She parked in front of her towering three-story brick house, next to my car. "Let me make it up to you. Come on in for a drink."

I cycled through my usual list of excuses but was too tired to think of one. "I'd like that."

"I think it's high time I told you what happened between us—all of us."

We walked inside and Roxy grabbed a bottle of wine and two glasses from the kitchen before giving me the royal tour of her former grand social statement–turned-duplex, replete with a long vestibule leading to a circular salon on the left, spiral staircase on the right. As we walked through the hallway, I admired the formal dining room, the kitchen with a wood-burning stove. Downstairs, the huge basement was carved into three separate living areas, each housing an individual bunk, leaky and drafty. The second floor had three bedrooms and a bathroom; the third floor boasted a low ceiling, a large closet, and an attic with a ramshackle bar. We cautiously stepped out of the attic window, braved the falling shingles, and inched our way to a circular landing area, almost like a parapet, covered with beer cans and cigarette butts.

"I think a Ford used to live here," she said, uncorking the bottle of wine.

"Are you renting this place?" I asked.

"Not technically—no." She poured two glasses, set one down in front of me. "Just between us? My parents bought it for me. College graduation present."

"The truck, too?"

"Well, that's a little more complicated." She drained her glass, checked text messages on her buzzing cell phone. "Harper and I dated in college. We met in a poetry class junior year. I fell in love with 'Lament for the Death of a Bullfighter,' and Harper fell in love with me." She poured herself another glass. "He was only in there to meet girls—he actually told me that on our second date. That should have been a red flag. Anyway, we were good for a while. We gave each other balance, I think."

I'd never thought of a partner as "balance," something to levy the weight of the person I wanted to become. "If you like Lorca's intensity, you should read Camus. He doesn't play with language as much, but the insights into materiality are striking."

Roxy ignored me. "Harper's not a . . . not a 'good' person. He's arrogant and entitled and thinks he's a lot smarter than he actually is. But that's what attracted me, unfortunately—I think I still mistake cruel for sexy, insecure for mysterious."

"It's a process."

She laughed. "Right. Anyway, after the rush wore off, that grace period when you both consume each other, I started getting bored. I was bored by his drinking, bored by him disparaging his close friends, bored more than anything else by his lack of ambition. He wanted to sit around and drink and fuck and complain—that's it."

"Sounds like suicide."

"What?"

"I'm sorry—go on."

"I think he picked up on it—my growing lack of interest. Selfish guys like that often do and just double down on their behavior. In this case, he didn't—he wanted to marry his longtime appreciation for sandwiches with my appreciation for Spanish poetry. We spent most of senior year planning the food truck. I think it was his way of trying to salvage the relationship without genuinely changing." She paused, ran her hands though her hair.

"Well, it worked out in a way, right?"

"Not like it was supposed to. After we graduated, he started drinking more and more, thinking as long as we had this thing together, everything would be OK. One night, we were out at this bar in Ann Arbor and I saw him get a number from some waitress. Maybe it was the backlog of stress or the fact I'd been beating off the advances of guys who were smarter than Harper, better looking, better people, but I called it off. I still wanted to go through with Lorca's Tortas because I'd already invested so much of my time in the design, the message, the mission . . . I don't know. I wasn't going to let him take the business and use it as a vehicle to be a fucking prick. I get most of our business, anyway. So here we are."

"OK," I said. "But to answer my question earlier—where'd you get the money?"

She glared at me. "Where'd *you* get the money when you bought it?"

"My severance check," I said. "From the community center."

She topped off her glass. "Harper's dad."

"That's ironic. He said something disparaging to his friend about the same thing at the bar."

"He's a liar. Another reason we're no longer together." She ran her hand down her tattoo sleeve, looked at it thoughtfully. "No, his dad used to own a fabricating shop."

My stomach turned. "In Ferndale?"

"I don't remember. He tried to explain it to me, once. I'm not sure he ever asked his dad what happened. It doesn't matter now."

I watched the wine leave a stream of red tears in my tilted glass. "What about Doug? He seems quite taken with you."

She snorted. "Just like there are guys like Harper, there are guys like Doug. Someone who thinks that just because they aren't like Harper, they *deserve* you. I always thought we were friends—we met freshman year in the dorms, watched Almodóvar films on rainy Friday nights. He's an excellent cook—there's no talking around that—and Harper and I wanted him on board. But the second Harper and I broke up he was at my doorstep with flowers." She shook her head.

"It's like it's our only value now, since no one can make any money."

"What do you mean?"

"With all the manufacturing jobs gone—jobs that my grandpa had. Just being alive and willing to work entitled you to a decent life."

"But don't you think it's stupid, in a way?" She poured another glass. "Mourning the loss of a dead way of life? It's dead—that's the whole point. Loving something that's dead isn't really love—it's mourning."

"I don't think it's dead."

She laughed, dipped her head forward, the way drunk people do. "You look so earnest when you talk like that." She picked up the bottle, motioned it toward me. "Sure you don't want some more?"

"Thanks, but I still need to drive."

She took a sip and swirled it around her glass. "I think most people drink, you know, *drink* drink, 'cause they want to forget something."

"I think we're too young to talk about forgetting," I said.

"Easy for you to say." She filled her glass again. "What did you want to do when you were young?"

"To work at the community center. To teach the kids to manufacture their own worlds until I met someone who would want to manufacture our own. Buy a house, fill it with kids, their sounds, all of us creating something unique."

She looked out onto the street, watched moths dance around the flickering streetlights. "The smell. I hated the smell of this place. No matter what you do, you can't get the fumes out of your nose, can't wash it from your hair. I wanted to live somewhere where no one's even heard of a fucking car—and if they did, it was something that dropped people off, took them away. Not some place full of machines and people who have make them, maintain them . . . let them rot, let them fucking rot." She took a sip from her glass, then looked back at me. "That's what I *thought* I wanted, when I was young. But then I thought—what if I stayed? What if I was part of the shift away from manufacturing to the New Economy?"

I reached for the bottle. "I'll take another glass of wine, actually."

"Speaking of manufacturing . . . there's something I've been meaning to talk to you about."

My phone buzzed—a number I didn't recognize. "Hello?" I asked as I answered.

Roxy continued, her voice lower, words measured. "We've been so popular that I've started researching the possibility . . ."

"Candy?" I didn't recognize the voice, either.

"May I ask who's calling?" I asked.

". . . for us to have a real brick-and-mortar . . ."

"It's Mrs. Baker . . . from across the street on . . . your grandpa just fell."

At Beaumont Hospital in Royal Oak, the doctors ran tests all night. At two in the morning, the doctor said he'd be fine—a deep bruise on his hip—but that it was time for the family to consider alternative options. My parents walked in an hour later, and the three of us sat in a cramped room lit by fluorescent light. The doctor handed us brochures for local nursing homes, then left us to talk.

"We can't take him," my mom said. "There's no hospitals close to us."

"I could," I said. My phone buzzed continuously: messages from Doug, Harper, and Roxy about their silly love triangle.

"It's a full-time job," my dad said.

"Really?" My face turned red. "I didn't know that." I stood up, trembling.

"Calm down," my mom said. "This is an emotional time for everyone."

"It's a nuisance for you, that's all it is." I grabbed the brochures from my dad's hands, threw them in the trash, and walked out to the parking lot.

My phone buzzed again—a call this time.

"I don't give a fuck! I don't care! Leave me the fuck alone!"

"Candy?" It was Suzanne.

"Suz," I said, choking back tears. "God, Suz . . . my grandpa . . ."

In October, after catering a football tailgate in the parking lot behind Wayne State's Adams Field, I drove my grandpa to American House, the nursing home on John R and Woodward Heights. "We don't have to do this," I said.

"Candy, if your great-grandfather lived to be my age, I wouldn't have wanted to spend my youth carting him around."

"You're not a burden," I said.

He smiled, held my hand.

Inside, a nurse gave us the tour. The "apartment" was nice enough—a large bedroom and bathroom—plus three decent-looking square meals and plenty of daily activities (grandpa was particularly drawn to the monthly trips to Comerica Park in the summer). I don't think it was fear I saw in my grandpa's eyes—more a resignation of being a child again, dependent on people who were paid to love you.

On the ride back to his house, we stopped at the liquor store and bought a six-pack of Stroh's bottles, drinking one each with the windows down. I wrapped the nursing home brochure around my beer, making a koozie.

"Just think about it," he said later as I moved him from his wheelchair to his bed, pressing a phone into his hand.

I kissed him on the forehead. "I'll try."

I was already thinking about tomorrow—the Halloween party we were catering in Roxy's West Village neighborhood, how early I had to be up to do all the prep work. Then my phone rang.

"So, when's your flight?" I said to Suzanne.

"I just landed. I'm at my parents'. They want to see you."

"You might have to come here. I don't want to leave him alone."

"Works for me. It's been forever since I've seen your grandpa."

I looked over at him, already asleep. "Another time. It's been a long day."

"I'll be over in ten."

She looked like all the pictures of actresses I saw in the celebrity magazines in the checkout lines at Kroger—lean, tan, stoic. And that made me self-conscious, in a way—my diet wasn't exactly replete with Vitamixed smoothies and vegan delicacies; something about the digestive nature of shame requires animal proteins. I nervously pinched the layer of fat above the waistline of my jeans.

I grabbed us two beers from the fridge and we walked into the backyard, the permanently wet autumn grass coated with a thin layer of curled brown leaves. I told her about my parents up north, how they left three years ago and hardly ever came back to visit. Suzanne told me her dad had invested his grandfather's trust money in real estate a little too liberally before the crash, and that after the money had dried up, sunk deeper and deeper into a "sustainable" gambling addiction, her mom deeper and deeper into increasingly large bottles of white wine.

"*The Fall of the House of Usher*?" I asked.

She laughed. "Something like that."

A flurry of cold wind scattered the leaves. "Tell me about *Dog Days*."

"I'll give you the pitch. Girl moves to post-crash Detroit to be with the guy she loves, but he dumps her for a career in Hollywood. So now she's all alone, and instead of wallowing in sorrow she sort of drifts from service job to service job, making new friends, going on awkward dates with guys who have been affected by the recession, and in the process, discovering how to live in a post-money economy, all while falling in love with Detroit." She smiled and looked at me. "Sort of *New Girl* meets *Little House on the Prairie*, set in the Rust Belt." She scratched her chin thoughtfully. "Which is considered chic these days, unfortunately. Hollywood seems fascinated by human residue."

"Who's playing the lead?"

"Kristen Stewart, if she's not busy with a feature."

"Poor casting choice," I said. "She looks nothing like me."

"Oh, please."

"And the title's a metaphor, I take it?"

"Well, the idea is to make it a four-year show, each season a, well, season. The first season's set in August, ergo . . ."

"I always thought you might make that *Space Jam* thing we always talked about."

She laughed—we used to watch *Space Jam* over and over, talking about how it was the high point of American culture. You know—Michael Jordan, Bugs Bunny, R. Kelly, Warner Bros. The glorious flaws of individuality against the mindless and utterly domineering brute force of the collective. "The crest of American capitalism. And then everyone wanted their things cheaper."

"It's better than it was. Here, I mean. For some people."

"I never knew why you were so hung up on this place, honestly. What's the point of playing in the ruins?"

"Solidarity," I said.

"Whatever that means, now."

"That's the motto of the business, actually."

"That's right—Lorca would be proud." She finished her beer. "Speaking of solidarity . . ."

"What?"

"You never held a grudge, did you?"

"About what?"

"Leaving. Me leaving."

"Oh, I don't know. I never blamed you. I would've . . . should've left, too. If I could've."

"That's the whole point of the show, honestly. Staying in something that's not healthy in a hostile place because you can always almost touch the thing you really want."

An hour later, I walked her out to her car. We stood in silence for a while, dead leaves drifting past our feet.

"You should come," she finally said.

"What?"

"Come visit me. I live right next to a United Way. They'd love you. You'd be perfect."

"I can't just . . ."

"This isn't home anymore." She looked up at the searchlights from another grand opening, another bar or restaurant, swimming across the autumn sky. "Not for me . . . not for you. You did the best you could."

"I can't just abandon . . ."

"He wants to be at that nursing home, right? You said so on the phone."

"He's just trying to push me away so I can 'be young,' whatever the fuck that means."

"Well, what do *you* want?"

I watched the searchlights intersect, then disconnect. "Not this."

She backed away toward her car door. "Listen, I can get you a plane ticket to come with me, just to visit and see if you like it. Let me know."

I hugged her again, then she walked to her car and drove away.

. . .

The Halloween gig was a party at some West Village mansion—Roxy's new boyfriend, apparently, a Grosse Pointe auto dealer scion whose "Drunk Night" parties were becoming increasingly talked about around Detroit as *the* thing to do on Friday night. That's why he bought the house—he'd used it for Drunk Night ("a rolling ironic bourgeois black-sheep rave," as Roxy called it) the previous spring. He liked it so much he bought it as a foreclosure for practically nothing and stripped bare what was left inside: the peeling late-forties wallpaper, the plush bedroom carpeting. It was a sarcophagus for industrial upward mobility, and now it played host to the offspring of its distant relatives.

We entered through the parlor-style doors out front with our sandwiches. Roxy adjusted her outfit—Lorca himself, replete with bow tie and pompadour—and looked over first at Doug, wearing a large fried egg with holes cut in the arms, then at Harper, who wore his normal outfit of a white V-neck and tight black jeans, altered only by the ironic inclusion of vampire fangs and red contacts, then finally at me, clad in one of my grandpa's old light blue Dynamic Fabricating work shirts. Then her mouth shifted into an affected scowl as she scanned the room, settling on the punk band on stage playing a sullen version of "The Monster Mash" as drinks spilled around them.

The crowd ebbed and flowed around the parlor room, mocking the kitschy decorations of drugstore tombstones and Jell-O brains, laughing at cynical jokes about politics, religion, working service jobs in the new bars and restaurants dotting the neighborhood. The windows were boarded with freshly sawed artisan oak from a new old-style hardware store down the street.

"Who are you supposed to be?" Some high-ponytailed guy next to me winked and scratched his arm—I made out tattoos of the *Spirit of Detroit*, the Fisher Building, Michigan Central Station.

"A proletariat," I said.

"You're strange." He lifted his plastic cup and drank greedily from it.

"What about you?" I asked him.

When I looked around the room, I saw that everyone was wearing children's costumes, their arms covered with tattoos so obscure and outrageous that I thought they must be the temporary kind the kids and I would to stick on each other during rainy summer days at the center.

"I don't do costumes," he said. "I'm not a child anymore."

I'd had this conversation a hundred times while working for Lorca's: sterile, aggressive questions while looking blankly at you, trying to coerce you into bed because of the fascinating way they made money.

I changed the subject. "What brings you here?"

"I work on the urban farm down on East Grand Boulevard with one of the band members. We're collective farmers, I guess you could say."

"So it's a, what . . . a kibbutz? A commune?"

"We sell most of it, actually. Anarcho-syndicalist farming." He lifted his torta. "Like the Catalans in the Spanish Civil War."

"So you don't hate the free market?"

"Can't hate the free market." He finished his drink, eyes settling on a young woman dressed as Little Red Riding Hood. "It, you know . . . it won."

Roxy walked up to us, pulled me aside. "Did you think it over? The brick-and-mortar?"

"Yeah," I said.

Her eyes opened wide waiting for my response.

"Give me till the end of the night. I might have a better . . ."

Roxy's boyfriend, dressed as a Gilded Age dandy, slid his arm around her waist, and pulled her into the crowd in front of the stage.

"Tell me after the party!" she said before she joined the entire congregation scrolling through their smartphones, some on personal websites, some on dating apps, some checking their checking accounts stuffed with the remnants of a dead relative's will.

And that's when it struck me: suicide.

No, I thought. Suicide was using my severance money on a fucking ice cream truck. I wanted to fail. I felt too guilty abandoning the kids.

No. No, no, no: that was rebellion. *This* was suicide. An economy that generates no jobs or money, that is funded not from banks but trusts bulging with the pilfered money of labor—an economy based solely on the embrace of materialism and the pursuit of pure pleasure by those who can afford it.

No, not that, either. That was delusion, to think that materialism could be transcended through laughter, through bullshit.

But the drinking around me mirrored the drinking I'd constantly seen from the parents of my children from the center after Dynamic closed, from the retirees trading stories at Kady's, from the crew of Lorca's Tortas every day after work.

On the dance floor, as people jerked around to silly interpretations of formerly rebellious music, the drinking escalated to pushing, halfheartedly hurled punches. I wondered what they could have to fight about, or for . . . if what I had done with American S'Cream was its own kind of fight—one I had entered gamely and left bruised.

No, I thought. It was all suicide.

I took off my apron, folded it, and placed it on the floor. I looked around the room. Roxy, Doug, and Harper were among the crowd, drinking, laughing, fighting. I slid out the back door. No one even noticed.

I drove up Woodward in the far-right lane, back to Ferndale. I parked in the abandoned lot of Dynamic Fabricating and wandered through the factories along Wanda. Back in this place, where my immediate family should have been, I dreamed with open eyes about how beautiful this place must have looked all those years ago.

I walked in the house to find my grandpa sleeping in front of the television. In my dresser, I removed the brochure for American House nursing home, my one-way ticket to Los Angeles falling onto the floor. I had a Popsicle from the freezer on the back porch, watching smoke rise from drums of burning leaves, and texted Roxy that I wasn't coming back—I had a new opportunity I couldn't afford to turn down.

The next May, I got a call from Roxy. She told me the renovations were finished. I told her I knew—I had sold my house to a young couple expecting their first child, and I had moved in with my grandpa to become his full-time caregiver, the only job I really wanted. I got to watch Dynamic Fabricating's transformation from my porch every night after putting my grandpa to bed: watched the dumpsters out front fill with seven years of abandoned waste, watched Doug apply a slick new black coat of exterior paint, watched their friends drink cases of beer as they put in new windows and mechanical loading dock doors. She invited me to the grand opening. I told her I'd love to come.

I hung up and watched the Tigers game, listening to my grandpa's rants about the bullpen, the corruption of TV revenue, the faded bliss of weekday games at the old Tiger Stadium in Corktown. At four o'clock, I wheeled him to Lorca's new space. He smiled and said, "This isn't so bad, is it, Candy?" He kissed my hand. "Kind of like being a kid again."

We took the scenic route down Nine Mile, past the rush hour traffic. Spring was almost over, and I could taste the humid air of the hot season creeping across the city. There had been a recent spate of entrepreneurship in town—people talked excitedly about the recession finally ending. I looked at the new vintage clothing stores selling defunct factory work shirts and garish bowling league polos, the record shops stocked with mint condition Rolling Stones vinyls, the trendy hair salons with their bright façades offering discounts on '50s era fades—the spirit that all new entrepreneurship has in that hopeful phase where anything seems possible. The shops waiting to be bought were scattered between them, soon to be filled by other retail businesses that employ a handful of people who don't really need to work but need to find something amusing on their one-way trip to dissolution. And when all those spaces are filled, I can imagine the aging workers from the factories that these buildings used to be, like veterans from a foreign war stopping and feeling the new materials and trying to remember how it was that they were able to buy their sliver of the American Dream before the memory's gone, reverted back to kitsch.

There was a small crowd inside Lorca's Tortas—close friends and family. Roxy had a navy-blue blazer over her revolutionary tattoo sleeve.

"I'm so happy you made it," she said, her voice lower, more assured. Her hair was straightened and parted. Doug smiled at me from the kitchen doorway. Over by the bar, Harper lifted his head and tipped an invisible cap in my direction.

"I wouldn't miss this for the world," I told her.

The space really was lovely—warm and open, filled with reclaimed tables and chairs, all immaculately finished by one of Roxy's friends at a new 1940s-style hardware store farther down Hilton Road.

Roxy gave us an informal tour, showing off the gleaming metal bar, the tables made from reclaimed wooden pallets. "There was a conscious decision to incorporate the history of the building into the new business," she said.

"History," my grandpa said.

"Seriously," Roxy said, reaching for my hand. "This wouldn't have happened without you. I still don't know why you left."

I squeezed her hand. "It doesn't matter now."

There was a shout from the kitchen. "I'll be right back," Roxy said.

As she walked toward the kitchen, I turned back toward the entrance, taking my grandpa with me. I walked outside and drank in the carbon fumes, squinted up at the sun, then turned to face the building and the huge pane of glass that used to serve as the window into the offices of Dynamic Fabricating, now a sleek portrait of a different kind of service.

Just then, the sun broke through the clouds, casting its five o'clock light on the windows. The inside disappeared, and I was faced with my own reflection. I played with the knots in my hair, smoothed out the wrinkles in my dress. Then, from behind me, people started coming into the picture, perfectly reflected in the window.

I began to pick out some of the faces in that gathering crowd: a tired man in a Goodwill blazer, résumé in hand; a woman clad in upscale corporate garb and her weathered father; a good-looking guy my age with a date who looked much older; a dirty landscaper, reeking of booze; four brothers wearing green soccer scarves over their cuts and bruises; an affectionate, affluent couple swinging their daughter between them;

a beautiful woman my age, wearing an unseasonable gray shawl that partially hid a psychology textbook; a hooded junkie nodding off on her feet; a steel-toed shopworker trailed by a mangy cat; four teenage boys, clearly high, passing out concert flyers; a couple leading a small group from the nursing home I couldn't put my grandpa in. I tried to make out the faces of my children or their families from the community center but couldn't find any. I knew they were all gone—their former homes now occupied and rehabbed by kids who looked like Doug and Roxy and Harper.

The crowd exchanged pleasantries—like my grandpa, many of them used to work here or knew someone who did. I overhead someone say, "You want to stay and eat something?" Another voice laughed. "This ain't my kinda place." And with that they all dispersed, their image in the window replaced by a larger crowd, all young, all grinning, tattooed and exquisitely coiffed, excited to be at the grand opening of the hottest new restaurant in town.

I wheeled us down to Kady's Bar.

To my surprise, the place was full—people lined the bar and the unsteady tables along the walls.

I ordered us beers, eavesdropped on conversations, as my eyes adjusted to the darkness:

"Inside looks good."

"Too clean."

"Too quiet."

When they did adjust, I saw the place was full of the same people from the opening—the same people from outside Lorca's Tortas.

"What's the starting wage for a server, anyway?"

"Two-fifty. Plus tips."

There was laughter.

"What's so funny?"

"It was fifteen at Dynamic."

"Two-fifty's better than nothing."

"Sure. Sure it is."

My eyes drifted toward one of the TVs. On it was an ad for *Dog Days*. Good for you, Suz. The early crowd from Lorca's Tortas, from Dynamic Fabricating, drank silently, everyone exchanging glances in tacit agreement that we could drink, laugh, or fight.

ACKNOWLEDGMENTS

Stories from this collection have appeared in the following publications: "Don't Let Them Win," in *The MacGuffin*; "Exit, Stage Left," in *Great Lakes Review*; "You're in the Wrong Place," in *Moon City Review*; "Acolytes," in *Midwest Review*; "Was it Good for You?" in *Storm Cellar*; "Easter Sunday," in *Third Wednesday*; "Memorial," in *Beecher's*; "Devil's Night," in *Clackamas Literary Review*; and "The Slow Death," in *Almost Five Quarterly*.

Thank you to my family—my parents, Dan and Laurie, and my twin sister Catherine, who always believed this book. Thank you to the Emerson College WLP program, especially Brian Malloy, the first person to encourage my fiction writing. Thank you to the Wayne State University English department—M. L. Liebler, Donovan Hohn, and especially Caroline Maun, the first person to read, edit, and take these stories seriously, and to push me to finish them. Thank you to the University of Minnesota MFA program: Julie Schumacher, Sugi Ganeshananthan, and Charles Baxter, for shaping and expanding both this book and the way I write. Thank you to all of the editors of the literary magazines these stories first appeared in for believing these stories were good enough to print. To the Gesell, Loughead-Eldregde and Jasina families: thank you for your financial support. And thank you, in the strongest possible terms, to Annie Martin, Emily Nowak, Jamie Jones, Carrie Downes Teefey, Kristina Stonehill, and the incredible team at Wayne State University Press for bringing this book into the world.

Special thanks to Todd and Lorin Woods for the informal summer residencies and endless nights by the pool; to Cass Corridor United ("no one likes us, we don't care"); to Jake, Chris, Scott, Michael, Dominic, Derek, Q, and the extended Rosiek family for so many incredible celebrations; to Hannah and Liana, genius and generous poets/ trivia masters; to Steve, Sal, and Drew, incomparable roommates and 64 opponents; to Ben, Mcgarry, Eli, Orson, and Aaron—keep producing inspiring work; to Alex, Mike, Gabe, Zack and Greg, for being my first and best friends; to Kat, for your intelligence, grace and humor; to Ye Olde Saloon, the greatest bar in the world. Lastly, thank you Detroit and its environs: the most beautiful place in the world.

ABOUT THE AUTHOR

Joseph Harris's stories have appeared in *Midwest Review, Moon City Review, Great Lakes Review, The MacGuffin, Third Wednesday, Storm Cellar*, and have received the Gesell, Tompkins, and Detroit Working Writers' Awards for fiction. He holds an MFA from the University of Minnesota, an MA from Wayne State University, and a BFA from Emerson College. He lives in Oak Park, Michigan.